THE PLAGUE *of* KOSMON

THE PLAGUE *of* KOSMON

Rise of the Seer, Book 3

Peter J. Rasor II

H. Alex Dennis, Illustrator

RESOURCE *Publications* · Eugene, Oregon

THE PLAGUE OF KOSMON
Rise of the Seer, Book 3

Resource Publications
An Imprint of Wipf and Stock Publishers
199 W. 8th Ave., Suite 3
Eugene, OR 97401

www.wipfandstock.com

PAPERBACK ISBN: 978-1-6667-3283-2
HARDCOVER ISBN: 978-1-6667-2696-1
EBOOK ISBN: 978-1-6667-2697-8

MARCH 15, 2022 2:34 PM

First, this book is dedicated to my lovely wife, Jennifer,
who has always believed in me and supported me.
Secondly, it is dedicated to my four lovely ladies
who have me wrapped around their little fingers.

"The only thing that consoles us for our miseries is diversion, and yet this is the greatest of our miseries. . . . But diversion amuses us, and leads us unconsciously to death."

–BLAISE PASCAL, *PENSÉES*, #171

Contents

List of Characters | ix

PART ONE: SEEK

1   THE DREAMER | 3

2   FATE | 11

3   THE PATH OF SEDEQ | 17

4   PETRA | 27

5   SUREK | 35

6   ABADDON | 43

7   SANGOMA | 49

8   PSEUDOMAI | 56

9   PHILO | 64

10   ZOE | 72

11   THE SCARLET RIDERS | 80

12   THE DUNGEONS | 87

13   THE SULTAN | 96

Part Two: Rise

14   Truth | 105

15   Escape | 114

16   The Journey | 122

17   The Donkey | 133

18   The City of Light | 142

19   The Plan | 152

20   Armageddon | 159

      Epilogue | 174

List of Characters

Abaddon – Also known as the Greater Power or Ruler of the Shadows, the nemesis of Lamlorde and the Speech

Elihu – The wise Seer and friend of Seikh

Dr. Ichabod – Scientian and Seikh's father

Lamlorde – The one prophesied by the Seers to hold the cure for the plague

Lucy – Transmutant and Seikh's mother

Philo – Scientian and Seikh's best friend

The Pravitas – Transmutants and servants of Sangoma

Pseudomai – The mysterious Seer who befriends Seikh

Sangoma – Necromancer and Surek's associate

Scarlet Riders – A division of Surek's army

The Scientian Race – Kosmonians who are known for being rational and scientific

The Seers – Kosmonians who are known for their dreaming and myths

Seikh – The young Kosmonian in search of his identity and purpose

The Speech – The nemesis of Abaddon

Surek – The Transmutant sultan of Kosmon

The Transmutant Race – Kosmonians who are known for evolving and changing their identity

Part One

Seek

Part One

Seek

1

The Dreamer

S eikh lay in his bed awake. He could hear Father and Mother speaking softly as they had the previous four nights. In hopes of making out any words being spoken, Seikh stared at his door and lay as still as possible, even holding his breath occasionally. The door had been left ajar by his mother after she tucked him in. Seikh's attempt to overhear their discussion was, as always, futile, as he could only hear the crackling of the fire Father had made to warm their old log home. Its dim light danced gracefully through the door's opening and slid gently under it. It seemed like hours had passed since Mother left the room.

The soft sound of their voices piqued Seikh's curiosity to the point that he could no longer ward it off. He knew they must be discussing something important. Void of any joviality, his parents' voices were somber, serious. Seikh was determined to find out what was being said, but he did not want to leave the warmth of his bed. The old log house he called home leaked in cold air from the dark night. As he bit the inside of his cheek in nervousness, he could stand it no longer. He had to know what was being said.

Slowly, Seikh wriggled out of his covers, slipped his feet onto the floor, and crept to the rickety door. Although the dark wooden slats of the floor creaked as he pranced, he successfully made it to the door without much noise. Father's and Mother's words became clearer as he perched closer to the glowing opening.

"I do not know what went wrong."

Father's voice was low, calm, and rather smooth. This is how all the voices of the Scientian race sounded. The tone was evidence of the

Scientian's cool and rational thought, or so it had always been said to Seikh. The Scientian appearance, however, could easily be perceived as ghastly. They were apeish, but with long, straight hair, and stood, on average, five feet tall. Despite their intimidating presence, it was said that the Scientians could and would never hurt a single person or race, as they were never given to fits of rage or emotion. They were not beastlike in their demeanor at all. They were utilitarian, seeking what was best for everyone, always thinking things through and never allowing themselves to believe in myths. Evidence and logic were their companions. Seikh's father was no different.

"I thought that the Scientians had this under control," Mother retorted, "that they had finally made a breakthrough—found a cure."

Mother's voice was more emotional, fit for the Transmutant race. The Transmutants were not always rational, it was said, but they were a gentle race, although their physical appearance could be just as deceptive as that of the Scientians. The Transmutants were a single race, but they would often take on various and unique forms, leaving the impression that their race was made up of different-looking creatures. Some appeared as apes, some as horses, and others even a mixture of animals. Most, if not all, evolved into different forms over the course of life. Seikh's mother had a head like that of a horse, though smaller and rounder. Off her chin hung a thin, long beard, and her skin appeared bluish in the light. The remainder of her physique more closely resembled the infamous ancient beings who had lived long ago.

The Transmutants could be indignant, and Seikh detected this in Mother's voice presently. She was demanding an explanation from Father about the cure. Seikh had heard all about the cure. Father, as one of the Scientians, had been commissioned to find a potion to wipe out the plague of Kosmon. The plague was said to be as old as Kosmon, the world of the Scientians, Transmutants, and "Dreamers." The plague seemed to infect everyone at some point in life, and it always led to death. The origin of the plague was unknown, just as it was said that the origin of Kosmon was unknown. However, just like a proverb, it was repeated that if anyone could find a cure, it was the Scientian race. They were, after all, the guarantors and true seekers of knowledge. If they could not find a cure, then no one could.

Father's reply to Mother, coming after a few moments of silence, seemed calculated and intentional. "The Scientians, as you know, dear, have been working on this for millennia. If we are to finally find a cure, my race must continue to work on it. We will find it. We will find it." His voice trailed off. "*We must give it more time.*" Seikh could tell by the wavering of Father's voice that he was puffing on his pipe, probably wearing his glasses and warming himself by the fire. "But now is *not* the time to quarrel," he continued more slowly. "We have just lost our one and only son to this plague. We must give time to mourning."

"Yes, I suppose you are right," Mother replied, her voice cracking. She began to sob. Within seconds and without warning her voice began to rise. If it had not been late at night, she would have easily been screaming in some fit of rage. But she was careful to keep her voice low while emphasizing every word. "But we all know who has been blocking the Scientians' progress—those Dreamers!" Mother struggled to find enough air for her next words. "They think they have a monopoly on the truth and how to eradicate this plague. Their outlandish stories of hope and unfulfilled promises! And that foolish talk—The Speech. They do not want any others to succeed in finding a cure! Who do they think they are, telling others what to do and think? Filling minds with hope, only to watch loved ones die. They all ought to be—"

"Yes, dear. Yes, dear. Come now. Settle down," Father replied in a couth tone. "You must not upset yourself and allow your emotions to get the best of you. In time, the Dreamers will suffer the consequences for their indoctrinating ways. We Scientians know their ways well—their myths, their fables—always living in their made-up dreams. Everyone does. We are working out a solution for them. Just be more rational, my dear, or else you are liable to succumb to the plague as our son did or perhaps evolve into something you wish not to become."

Father's words momentarily appeared to have settled Mother. The light from the fire was dimmer than before, and the cold of the night seemed more piercing. Seikh felt his heart pounding in his chest, and he thought perhaps he could even hear his blood rushing through his veins. The conversation aroused such anxiety in him that he could not think. He could only feel. Mother's hideous tone especially frightened him. It was almost as if Mother had in fact evolved—at least temporarily—into something beastly. Seikh had heard about others mutating into a different form but had never witnessed the transformation itself—Mother had always made sure of that. She was his protector. Though he could not presently see into the room where Mother and Father spoke, Mother's angry, emphatic words made it feel like she was morphing into something—something hideous.

A few moments later, Seikh came back to his senses, and he heard his mother sobbing again. This time more gently. *No*, thought Seikh. *Mother has not evolved into something monstrous. Not tonight. Mother was just upset.*

"There, there," Father remarked calmly.

Complete silence settled in the old log house. Seikh could smell smoke, indicating that the fire must have gone out. He began to feel uneasy. He wondered if Mother would come check on him to make sure he was covered. She had always did this on cold nights ever since he was a small child. Mother loved him and always showed it. To avoid being detected, he quickly yet softly slipped back into bed. The venture to the door had made him quite cold and so the warm bed was very welcoming. His covers made a small cave in which to hide the anxiety that was aroused by Father's and Mother's conversation.

A stream of questions came at once to Seikh as he laid there, warming his feet and hands, shaking from the cold but perhaps also from fear. *What did Mother mean that their only son had died from the plague? I'm their only son, but I'm not dead.* He looked at his hands closely and rubbed them together to affirm his existence. *The plague hasn't killed me.* Did they have another son? Did he have a brother? Wasn't *he* their only son? Seikh was confused, bewildered. All in a single moment his life came into question. Like lightning striking a tree, his heart was split in two with questions about who he was. *Are Mother and Father my parents? Where am I from?* It was too much for Seikh's mind to grasp.

Mother's indignation and rage against the Dreamers unsettled Seikh. He did not know much about the race of Dreamers. He had always been told to stay away from them, to keep his distance, and that they were trouble. He always trusted his mother about this. He loved her above all else.

Seikh never personally observed anything troubling about the Dreamers. This was probably because he never had any real contact with them. His only experience with a Dreamer was years ago as a very young child. He remembered playing one warm summer in the woods—the Woods of Ebony—in which his house was nestled. A single ray of sunlight peeked through the trees, lighting upon a tall figure in the distance. The figure stood about six feet tall and had long, gray hair on its head and face. The figure seemed mysterious and gave the appearance of floating when it walked. It was dressed in long white and copen blue rags. The figure appeared to have been kind, consoling a Transmutant child who was sitting on an old tree stump and weeping. The only odd thing that stuck out in Seikh's mind about seeing the Dreamer is that it looked like he had transformed the Transmutant child into a different creature with the touch of his hand. The child had quit crying, and the Dreamer looked up from her and caught a glimpse of Seikh. Seikh ran home and told Mother what he saw. She told him that the figure he had seen was a Dreamer and that Dreamers tried to fool people with magical tales that they dreamed up. According to Mother, Seikh was to avoid "it," the Dreamer, altogether.

This night, after listening to Mother and Father, Seikh thought he began to understand what was so troubling about the Dreamers: they were impeding progress of a cure for the plague. Certainly, such actions were uncalled for and demanded shunning. They preferred loved ones to die, as Mother had said. But it seemed so confusing that they would be in opposition to the cure. The picture of the Dreamer consoling the child in Seikh's mind did not seem to match the one Mother painted with her words, but he was to trust his mother. She cared about him and loved him above all else. She would never lie to him. That's what she had told him, and this is what all good Kosmonian boys believed about their parents.

One thought followed another as Seikh lay in his bed. His hands and feet were no longer cold, and he found himself drifting off to sleep.

Seikh was soon hurled into a dream he had dreamed many times before. This time, however, was different. It felt more real. It felt like he was really *there* in his dream, as if he had been carried into it. And he *knew* he was there. The colors of everything were rich, and the sounds were clear and distinct. In fact, Seikh believed he could actually smell things. The impression was that the dream was actually occurring to him—he was *living* it.

The dream began as it had many times before. Seikh was seated in what appeared to be a large dining hall. In the middle of the room stood a long, narrow table that stretched from end to end. Strangely, the opposite end of the table from where Seikh was seated could not be seen, for it trailed off into the dark. The only light in the room was given off by large golden candelabras that were set in a row down the middle of the table from one end to the other.

The table had the whitest tablecloth Seikh had ever seen, and it was set with every kind of food imaginable. It was more appetizing than anything Seikh had ever seen or desired. It was as if the smell of the food dripped with sweetness and the color of it could speak, reeling in, even dragging, his appetite into its very essence. *This is a banquet for kings and queens,* thought Seikh.

As interesting as the table and its setting were, the creatures seated around the table intrigued Seikh more. They did not appear as creatures at all, at least not ones he was used to seeing. Rather, the creatures had similar features, except there were two distinct types. One type had longer hair that flowed from the top of its head down its back, and it was slenderer than the other type. The type with the shorter hair had more muscle and spoke like Father—calmly but deeply. Both, however, had a feature that stood out the most: smooth skin, similar to his own, but without hair. They were all dressed in fine clothes like one would wear to a wedding banquet.

The creatures appeared very jolly. They engaged in conversation, laughter, and the consumption of food. Every creature was smiling. There was no sadness or dullness. Off in the distance it sounded as if stringed instruments were being played, adding to the joyful, spirited occasion.

Up to this point, the dream was identical to the other ones Seikh had dreamt, except for the vividness of it. But then came an odd twist: Seikh was just a bystander in the midst of the party. He sat watching the creatures partake in the banquet, and it seemed to last forever.

Then one of the creatures with long hair turned and made eye contact with Seikh. It motioned for him to come to the table. At first, fear gripped Seikh as he was not sure he should go. Was it safe? But then he managed to convince himself it would be acceptable for him to join the creatures—they looked lovely after all.

As Seikh approached the table, the creature pulled out a chair and patted it. The chair was plush and red, and it was trimmed in gold. It matched all the other chairs. The smell and color of the food was even more intense and desirable than it had been from farther away. Seikh could barely contain himself. As he sat in the chair provided for him, he hesitated to begin eating the food set before him, but then a voice (it was difficult to tell from where it came), spoke emphatically but kindly: "Take. Eat. It is good."

Seikh surveyed the food, chose a piece of juicy meat, and placed it on his tongue. The flavor was unimaginable. The meat seemed to melt in his mouth. He closed his eyes and savored it.

Upon opening his eyes to have another delightful bite, Seikh looked around at the creatures, studying each one. He began to understand why they were so happy. The food was like none other. At the thought of another bite, Seikh's appetite welled up like a fountain and he could no longer re-strain himself. His self-control fled like a bird after its prey. Thrusting both hands into the food around him he gorged himself, and joy filled his heart like never before. He ate without knowing how much time had passed.

The creatures around the table accepted him as if he were family. Seikh found the conversations full of life and wonder. The creatures told fasci-nating stories. They spoke of adventures in a world he was not acquainted with, but it didn't seem to matter. Everyone enjoyed himself.

The food was more succulent than any he ever had. And the more he ate, the more he wanted. The more he wanted, the more food appeared on his plate as from nowhere. It was quite miraculous. As Seikh finished one scoop of vegetables, more would appear. Before he was finished with his meat, more would already be on his plate. The food never ran out. Seikh had never been so satisfied in his life. He didn't want to leave the company of his new family nor give up the food. He felt at home like he never had before. He wanted to live this dream and never leave or wake up.

But as good things always seem to come to an end, the dream began to change. As Seikh finally began to feel full from eating, a mysterious-looking figure appeared from the darkness from the other end of the table. It was a creature dissimilar to, but not entirely unlike, the ones seated at the table. It was quite beautiful, stood tall and straight, and it resembled a Dreamer. It had long hair on its head and face, but its appearance was one of bril-liance, which contrasted with the lackluster appearance of the Dreamers in Kosmon. It emitted a glorious light from within itself. The creature had similar features to those around the table—hands, face, and presumably legs and feet.

The creature was carrying what looked like a silver platter with a cover, and the cover had a lock on the side. The creature promenaded toward the table. The music was no longer playing, and no one was laughing or speak-ing. It was completely silent, with all eyes fixed upon the majestic figure. The creature, reaching into the pockets of his robe, gently and slowly pulled out a key. He placed the key into the lock on the platter and turned it. The click of the lock echoed throughout the banquet hall as it opened. As the creature opened the platter's cover, a waft of tender, juicy meat filled the room. As it slid the cover off the platter, the creature announced, "Take. Eat. It is very good. The best I have saved for last." The voice sounded familiar to Seikh. It sounded similar to the voice he had heard earlier when sitting at the table, but something about it made Seikh uneasy, even suspicious that something was not right.

The creature sat the platter of meat onto the table and immediately everyone began to take some and eat. The platter was passed and not one refused. In fact, everyone thrust his hands into the meat and ate it like animals. When the platter came to Seikh, he too became overwhelmed by the aroma and fell face forward into the meat and ate some. The creature next to him suddenly pushed him and seized the platter. The creature who had been ever so pleasant before was no longer smiling, but instead had the worst grimace on its face. It grunted at him, "Give me some! Why are you withholding it from me?"

Seikh began to tremble. He looked to his left and then around the table. The creatures were attacking the meat and consuming it as if no more would be provided. Juice from the meat stained the white tablecloth while the creatures tore into the meat even more, yelling and grabbing at one another.

The scene was ghoulish. The light that once glimmered beautifully from the candelabras faded, leaving only a soft blue hue throughout the room. The creatures around the table began to mutate into unsightly, haggard, feral beasts. Seikh would have sworn that he even saw many of the creatures change into Scientians and Transmutants, at least for a split second. The oddity was that through the entire transformation, the creatures continued to eat the meat and want more. It seemed as if it was the meat that was making them what they were becoming. Seikh found himself doing the same—eating and wanting more although his stomach was about to burst.

Seikh's arms began to feel as if an electrical charge were running through them. He looked down at them slowly. They were changing and becoming brown and then gray, with hair growing to unimaginable length. Fright gripped him. As he sat amid the commotion and ravenous sounds of the beasts, with the noise only getting louder and more violent, he began to scream. He then heard the voice again.

"Seikh. Go and Find!"

Within seconds Seikh awoke, sitting straight up in his bed, sweating and breathing fast and hard. The light from the fire Father had made was gone and his room around him was dark. Mother and Father could no longer be heard.

2

Fate

Seikh sat in his bed, anxious and worried. *Only Dreamers dream,* he thought. *What if someone finds out that I dream? Maybe, somehow, I am one of . . . them?*

The thought was frightening. Surely, he wasn't a Dreamer. All he knew was that he must make sure never to tell anyone of his dreams, especially *this* dream.

As he gained his composure, he heard numerous voices coming from far away. They were faint and he could not make out exactly where they were coming from. The loghouse itself was dark and quiet and, it appeared, sound asleep. Seikh's eyes jumped to the window at the end of his room. Were the voices coming from outside?

Arising from his bed, he tip-toed to the window, which was clothed with heavy, dark drapes. A small sliver of moonlight peeked through the break in the drapes. He pulled them back slowly and slightly, wishing to remain unseen.

The window was frosted over from the cold night. Seikh breathed onto it and rubbed it with his hand, cleaning a spot to see out. He peered out, and he could see a crowd that had gathered in the Hinnom Meadow just beyond the trees. The Meadow, which stood in the midst of the Woods of Ebony, was about a hundred yards from the front of his house. A yellowish glow from numerous torches filtered through the trees from the crowd.

Seikh quickly turned away, slipped on his sandals, put on the rough-woven cloak that rested on the back of his chair, and then slipped out into the dark room where Mother and Father had been speaking. The house was deadly quiet. Seikh had a strong sense that the house was empty. He looked across the room and saw Mother's and Father's bedroom door open, their room utter darkness. Seikh was alone. *Where could they have gone?*

Seikh slowly made his way to the front door. He reached for the cold iron handle, gradually turned it, and the handle creaked until the door unlatched and popped open. Cautiously, Seikh slipped out into the night.

As he tiptoed through the woods, Seikh breathed slowly, creating a mist as he exhaled into the frigid air. The ground was frozen hard, and his feet felt the coldness. Wrapping his cloak around him, Seikh inched his way toward the crowd that had gathered in the meadow. He crouched closer and closer to the ground as he went, so as not to be seen. At last, Seikh was at the edge of the woods where the meadow began, which placed him only a stone's throw from the crowd. As he peered around a large tree he saw that a crowd of Transmutants and Scientians had gathered, surrounding a group of Dreamers. The Dreamers were tied to wooden posts, and they were all blindfolded. The crowd hurled names and accusations at the Dreamers. This was not just any crowd—it was an *angry* mob.

"These Dreamers must pay!" shouted a voice. "They are impeding progress! They are against a cure just so they can have power over us!"

"They have provoked our world to violence long enough!" screamed a Transmutant. "And they have spread their myths for the last time! No more! No more offenses, and no more of this intolerant Speech!"

Seikh spotted Mother and Father standing on the perimeter, to the left of the mob. Father was chiming in, but Seikh could not make out what he was saying. He could, however, hear Mother jeering.

"They must no longer live! They are to blame for the death of my son!" She was clearly wailing and doing her best to form her words. "They have judged others, and now judgment must come upon them! Kill them all! They killed my son!"

Just then, Father made his way into the middle of the mob and stood on a tree stump in front of the Dreamers. He motioned with his hand for the mob to quiet down. It was difficult to settle them, but after a few minutes, Father seemed to get their attention.

"My fellow citizens of Kosmon," he said in a loud-yet-calm voice. "You know well that we Scientians have for some time been trying to find a cure for the plague that curses all of us—the plague that induces violence in us and has led to the death of our parents, children, and loved ones—and even to the death of my only son . . ." Losing composure, Father's voice trailed off.

A voice interrupted. "Why should we listen to you when you had a son of a Dreamer in your own house? You're just as guilty!"

"Yeah, maybe you are in league with them!" shouted another voice.

The crowd erupted in jeers and began to chant, "Burn him too! Burn him too!"

It was evident that Father was dismayed and immediately humbled. He descended from the stump and another Scientian mounted it, motioning with his hand for them to be quiet. Once the crowd was calm again, the Scientian addressed them. "My friends, I understand your outrage. But there is no reason to turn on a fellow citizen of Kosmon, especially a rational and fact-loving Scientian like Dr. Ichabod. Yes, he took in a Dreamer's son some years ago. But this ought not be held against him—at least not at this moment. Besides, this is not an issue to be discussed presently. Remember what provoked this gathering tonight in the first place, the passing of Dr. Ichabod's son." He motioned toward Father as if to pay homage, and then he nodded at Mother. "And, Lucy, our thoughts are with you as well."

Seikh recognized that the Scientian speaking was none other than Dr. Kain, the leading Scientian in the attempt to find a cure for the plague. Father had worked with him for numerous years.

"We are gathered here to address the judgment upon the Dreamers who are presently before us." Dr. Kain paused, took off his glasses that gently laid at the tip of his nose, and continued. "We Scientians have discussed for many years what ought to be done with the Dreamers. We even spent many sleepless nights mulling over the appropriate action to take. And tonight, with the passing of Dr. Ichabod's *adopted* son," he emphasized, "we felt it prudent and necessary for the sake of the survival of Kosmon to arrest and bring before you every Dreamer we could find. We believe we have found all of them—except the one they call Lamlorde," he began to chuckle, "if this mythological creature exists at all."

The mob laughed with him while he attempted to gain control over his chuckling, which had turned into a fit of coughing.

"Thus," he continued after composing himself, "I bring before you this night these Dreamers." He waved his hand over the tied-up Dreamers who stood quietly behind him. "And I ask you to make a judgment, once and for all, on whether to condemn them to death for their crimes, not just for their everyday intolerance, condescension, and tall tales, but for obstructing the progress of finding and developing a cure for the plague. In essence, for inciting violence that has led to the death of multitudes of our loved ones."

The crowd began to get restless. "And," he began slowly and emphatically, "for attempting to resurrect the outlawed Ancient Order."

Whispers and chatter began simmering among the crowd, which then boiled up into hoots and hollers. Dr. Kain raised his voice over the crowd.

"Yes. You heard me correctly. We Scientians have ascertained that the reason the Dreamers have been obstructing the development of a cure is because this is their means to reestablish the Ancient Order. We must not allow this to happen. You know well the history of the Ancient Order—how oppressive it was and how it demanded obedience from every one of us. It was slavery. It was a web of lies, of dreamed up ideas, devised to hold back the progress of Kosmon, to bring about what we have nearly accomplished to this present day—the peaceful Eschatolis—a Kosmon without violence and the plague." Dr. Kain paused and then remarked slowly, "And, so, based upon these accusations, what say ye?"

The mob was incited once again, and it began to chant, "They must die! They must die!"

Dr. Kain motioned with his hand. "Now, now, now. We must be orderly about this. We must decide democratically and rationally whether they are guilty as charged. For those *in favor* of condemning the Dreamers to death for their crimes of inciting violence leading to the death of our loved ones and for conspiring to resurrect the Ancient Order, say, 'Yea.'"

"Yea!" belted out the entire crowd as a single voice.

"For those *not* in favor, say, 'Nay.'"

Seikh, who was now standing on the outskirts of the crowd in plain view, calmly yet confidently pronounced the word, "Nay."

Why he voted "nay" he did not know. In fact, he had no idea how he had moved from behind the tree to just outside of the crowd. During Dr. Kain's entire monologue he had felt drawn into the event, like his dream earlier, and he felt invisible to those around him. Yet, it was clear he was not. With Seikh casting the one and only vote not to condemn the Seers, the mob took immediate notice of him.

"You! Who are you?" cried a voice. A few of the Transmutants turned their torches to see who it was. Some noticed Seikh right away. "It's Ichabod's little Dreamer!" some cried.

"Impossible!" cried another. "He's dead!"

Gasps spread throughout the crowd. Chaos erupted. The mob began yelling and jeering. "Get him! Tie him to the poles with the others!"

Other voices cried out, "Get Dr. Ichabod and his wife! They're conspirators!"

Some of the crowd dragged Seikh's mother and father to the poles and tied them up. Other Scientians did their best to stop it, but the mob was out of control. "The ancient dreaming Seers will finally be no more!" yelled a voice in the distance.

The mob began running toward Seikh, and he spun around and dashed back into the woods, barely escaping the mob's grasp. As he did so, out of the corner of his eye he saw some of the mob using their torches to light up the Dreamers, along with Mother and Father. Others continued running after Seikh. He ran as fast as he could, jumping over tree branches and brush that lined the ground.

Upon entering the woods, he heard a voice that sounded familiar, "Seikh, turn right."

It was a low and gentle voice, yet firm, much like the voice he had heard in his dream. Suddenly a tunnel appeared before him. It was like a glass window that was smeared and distorted along the edges and clear in the middle where Seikh was running. The tunnel appeared to be guiding him through the woods and transporting him at the same time. A great sound of rushing wind arose as he ran.

After racing about fifty yards, the voice spoke again.

"Turn left."

He turned left. As long as he obeyed the voice, the tunnel guided and moved him through the woods. Seikh had no idea where he was going, and he began to be frightened. *Why am I listening to and obeying this voice?* he thought through his puffing. He decided to make his own decision where to go, and the tunnel disappeared, and the crowd began to get closer to him. Then the voice spoke again, "Seikh, trust me. I am your Protector. Turn left."

Observing that the crowd was now even closer, Seikh obeyed the voice. The tunnel reappeared and, in a flash, he was transported farther away from the crowd pursuing him. He could hear the crowd getting farther away. When Seikh looked back, he could no longer see the crowd. It had disappeared into the woods. No voices could be heard anymore.

When Seikh faced forward again, he noticed the tunnel was now gone, and he was running rather slowly. He felt his legs give out and he fell to his knees and then landed flat onto the ground. He felt faint, and he closed his eyes and fell asleep.

3

The Path of Sedeq

When Seikh awoke, he found himself in tall yellow-and-green grass. As he lifted himself from the ground, he noted that the Woods of Ebony were not far behind him. The air smelled simultaneously like life and death—like spring, with a fresh scent of earth and budding flowers, with an occasional scent of rotting trees and leaves mixed in. A few bees hummed around him. No sun shone. The sun never shone in Kosmon. But the light that filled Seikh's surroundings was brighter than usual.

Seikh was groggy and his thoughts muddled. His mind wandered back to Mother and Father and the image of the torches that gleamed in the night that set them and the Dreamers ablaze. Tears welled up in his eyes and he began to sob uncontrollably. Mother and Father were gone. He heard the echoes of the mob in his head about the Dreamers' hidden motive to bring back the Ancient Order, and the invective titles "Dr. Ichabod's little Dreamer" and "adopted son." *What is this "Ancient Order" and why was I called such a hideous name? Adopted? What is this all about?*

Seikh's racing thoughts were interrupted by a soft and gentle noise. He sat up and peered over the tips of the grass. He saw a narrow, winding river. It was shallow, and rocks protruded above the surface of the flowing water. Immediately on the other side of the river, along its banks, was an opening to a cave embedded in the side of an incline. Beyond the cave were gray trees that slowly became white at their topmost branches. The trees lined the riverbed like a seam. It was the Woods of Ivory. Seikh had heard about the Woods of Ivory only in stories that were considered folklore. The tunnel must have brought him a long way out from the Hinnom Meadow, for he was at the place where the Woods of Ebony ended and the Woods of Ivory began. The place where the dark met light was not folklore after all. It was real, and it was something mysterious for Seikh to behold. *I must be miles from home,* Seikh thought. He had never been so far from home.

He saw a dim light flicker at the mouth of the cave. A head appeared and beady eyes stared at Seikh from out of the dark opening. It was a Dreamer! The head called out to him, "Seikh! I have been expecting you. Come! We have much to discuss."

Just as quickly as the head had appeared, it faded back into the cave.

Cautiously, Seikh made his way to the opening. The Dreamer was waiting for him, standing straight as a board with his two hands folded on top a long, narrow, dark cane that looked like two snakes curled around each other. The Dreamer peered at Seikh when he entered. Seikh felt like the Dreamer was looking right through him, yet the gleam in his eye was welcoming.

Without moving a muscle, the Dreamer spoke. "I have been waiting for you. You must journey with me today and we must talk."

"But you are a Dreamer," Seikh began, "and—"

"And Dreamers are not to be trusted," the Dreamer interrupted.

"Yes. Mother and Father always told me—"

"Not to have anything to do with Dreamers," he said, finishing Seikh's sentence. He moved his head slightly. "Yes, I know what you have been instructed about 'Dreamers' as they call us."

Seikh was frightened of him. He wasn't sure whether to run or stay. "I thought the Scientians had arrested all the Dreamers. How did you get away? Do they know you're here?"

"I have my ways." The Dreamer paused. "Or should I say my ways are had? Eh?" He chuckled a bit. "And I have no idea if those Scientians know of my whereabouts."

Seikh thought a moment. "How do you know my name? And how is it that you have been expecting me?"

The Dreamer relaxed his posture, turned around, and began slowly walking further into the cave. "If you journey with me today, you will learn much."

The chit-chat and the terse answers were beginning to irritate Seikh. He was the impatient kind, always wanting to get to the point.

"Two things for starters," Seikh replied indignantly. "First, why should I journey with you? How do I know you will not do something to me? And second, Mother always told me there is really nothing to learn. Knowledge is created from our own experience, not discovered. How could you teach me anything?"

The Dreamer turned and peered at Seikh, lowered his voice, and said, "I see you take after both your mother and father. Both rational and irrational—and at the same time! Contradiction, I tell you! Tell me, young Seikh: If knowledge is created, why do you ask so many questions? Why not just project your own ideas and create answers for yourself, eh?"

The Dreamer's answer made Seikh uncomfortable, yet there was something satisfying about it. It seemed to make at least a little sense. The Dreamer was quiet for a few moments as he sat down on a large stone. Seikh crept further into the cave, and the Dreamer began softly.

"You might as well journey with me today. There is nowhere else for you to go now. They will be searching for you, and you will be safe with me—at least for a while. I know *your* name, so I might as well introduce myself." He stuck out his hand. "I am Elihu."

Seikh didn't return the favor of the handshake. Instead he sat down on both his hands on a rock across from him. "How do you know me?"

"Hmm," Elihu muttered. "There are many things I know, or shall I say which have been revealed to me?" He took his staff and began to poke at the floor of the cave and then stood up. "You must know the things I have to say to you. You must journey with me today. You have been sent to me for this reason."

Elihu, who had stood and was now towering above Seikh, made him feel quite small. He looked up at him. "But how do I know that you will not hold me captive and then kill me like you have done to so many of the children of Kosmon?"

Elihu scrunched down, looked Seikh in the eyes, pulled him close with both his hands, and whispered, "You do not really believe those stories about the Dreamers as told by the people of Kosmon, do you? Far be it from me if I were to do such a thing! I don't think you believe those stories, eh?" He stood up, letting go of Seikh. "If you truly believed them, you would not have voted 'nay' for my brothers."

Trembling, Seikh responded, "That's just it! How do you know things like *that*?"

"I know all about you, Seikh, son of a Seer."

Seikh looked at him, confused.

"Yes, son of a *Seer*. That's what we were called before this derisive name 'Dreamer' came along. I have watched you since you were a young child. I can tell you more of that at a later time, but for now, I will tell you about everything you seek answers to—if you will journey with me." Elihu paused and squinted. He seemed bothered. Turning, he began walking slowly further into the cave until he looked over his shoulder. "Come. Follow me, if you want to know the truth."

"Truth?" quipped Seikh. "Whose truth? Yours? The Scientians'? The Transmutants'? You speak as if you alone hold the truth—as if you expect everyone to bow down to your ideas. You are all the same—forcing *your* truth on others," he said, repeating words he had heard his mother speak.

Elihu then replied in a perturbed manner, "Ah, I see we are back to where we began. How long are you going to play this game, Seikh? How long are you going to be a blasted, irrational fool? Truth does not lie within *you*." He poked his staff a few times into Seikh's chest. "It is something *discovered*. You betray your own understanding of truth by simply asking me questions. If you hold your own truth, Seikh, why not provide answers to your own questions? Truth, my friend, must be loved above all else. But you are making it something unrecognizable and unlovable." He paused and took a deep breath. "Perhaps this whole thing is in vain. Maybe you are not the one The Speech spoke of. You are a stubborn old mule, pretending to be most reasonable and then playing tricks with the truth when it's right under your nose," he said, punctuating these final words with a tap of his staff on Seikh's nose. "Confound it! Remain in your contrived reality. Leave and become the slave Kosmon wants you to be. It's no matter to me!"

He abruptly turned and headed into the darkness of the cave.

Fear gripped Seikh with the thought of the Scientians and Transmutants catching up with him. "Wait! Don't leave me here. Tell me where I should go to hide from those who seek my life. It is now the light of day, and they surely will find me."

"Well, now, again you are speaking more reasonably, son." He chuckled. Seikh could not see him at first, but then a small flame pierced the darkness and he could see Elihu holding a torch. "Follow me and I will tell you everything you need to know. There is only one thing that can keep you safe now. And I will disclose it to you."

Seikh felt there was no other option. He desperately needed help and he needed answers. Who else was going to help him? Maybe this Dreamer could be useful after all. Everyone else wanted him dead, but the Dreamer didn't seem to.

Just then Seikh heard a faint rustling of tree leaves from behind him, and then distant voices. He turned and peered into the woods but saw nothing. The voices became louder with every passing second, and the sound of a crowd trudging through the leaves became distinct.

"Yes, Seikh. The sounds you hear are the ones who ran after you last night. They will continue to look for you until they find you, just like all the Dreamers—except me, of course. I was more protected this time around. Now that it is light out, they will have a full company searching for you." The Dreamer looked out into the woods. "Come with me now, or the voices we hear in the distance will find us soon."

Seikh solemnly looked at Elihu over his shoulder. "Will you keep me safe from them?"

"I shall, or my name is not Elihu."

Elihu led Seikh further into the dark cave. The walls began to encroach upon them on each side and the light from the mouth of the cave dimmed before eventually disappearing. Elihu's torch illuminated the path that descended and wound back and forth for what seemed like miles. Elihu kept a brisk pace, never once looking back to check on Seikh. They eventually stopped to rest upon stone benches carved into the walls. Elihu drew some water out of a basin that was cut into the rock wall.

"Here. We will rest a minute." Elihu's words were drawn out, and Seikh detected he was tired from the walk.

"Where are we?" Seikh inquired.

"We are on the Path of Sedeq. It will take us home."

"Home? Whose home?"

"First, to the home of the Dreamers. Beyond that, it leads to the Woods of Ivory. And beyond that . . ." Elihu stopped speaking and got a twinkle in his eye. He seemed to be overcome momentarily by unspeakable joy. It was an awkward moment for Seikh. "Beyond that? Well, let's just say, *home.*"

The word seemed to fall from Elihu's lips as if he just had a bit of honey.

"The Dreamers live in this cave?" asked Seikh.

"Yes. Well, they did until last evening, eh? We Dreamers have lived here since we were driven underground about three hundred years ago, after the Scientian War." Elihu, who had been staring at the floor, looked up at Seikh, perplexed. "You don't know about the war, do you?"

"I have heard about many wars, but never the Scientian War." Seikh was still somewhat uncomfortable with Elihu and suspicious of his stories. He could still hear in his mind the words of Mother, about how he shouldn't trust Dreamers. "Is it one of those mythological wars that we read about in the books?"

"No, no, no," Elihu replied. "It was a war that was unlike most wars. There were not many weapons, really, not physical ones anyway. The Scientians defeated the Ancients rather deceptively, which paved the way for the Transmutants to invade Kosmon and dispel what Ancients were left. They were very cunning, indeed, those Scientians."

"Nonsense," interrupted Seikh. "Mother and Father were right about you Dreamers."

"What is this you say?"

"The Scientians declaring war? They would never do such a thing. They are the most rational in Kosmon, and they are pacifists. They think through everything and would never take an action that would lead to war. And who are these Ancients you speak of? The only Ancients I have ever heard about are the mythological ancient beings in books who lived thousands of years ago. Everyone knows they were not real. They were invented to make sense of what the ancient Kosmonians could not understand by rationality and logic."

"Oh, how I wish it were true that the Scientians could never declare war!" exclaimed Elihu as he stood up. "What did you witness last evening? Who put your mother, father, and all the Dreamers to death? Only the Transmutants? No, I say. The Scientians! Just as they put to death all the Ancients. You think that the Scientians would never kill? Who chased you through the woods last night? Who is looking for you this very moment?"

Elihu now hovered over Seikh like a tree. He became calm and then gently spoke again.

"As far as the Ancients are concerned, they were real, sure enough. You will learn, Seikh, that much of what Kosmon tells you is mythological is actually true, or should I say *really real*, and what it tells you is true is in fact mythological. You better wake up from your dark dream and open your eyes to the light before it's too late." He turned and began walking down the path. "Come. It's surely near midday. We have far to go, and I'm already hungry from the walk. Soon you will be too, if you are not already."

The words "dark dream" fell like a weight upon Seikh's chest. He couldn't help but think of the dream he had the night before—the creatures which sat around the banquet table and how they were so welcoming and friendly—until the piece of meat was brought out which seemed to bring out the worst in them. Seikh's mind dwelled on the dream as Elihu led them down the Path of Sedeq, and he began to lag behind.

"Can't keep up, eh? Distracted by something are you?"

"I was just thinking," Seikh responded somewhat wearily.

"Ah. Something you learned to do from your father and not your mother, I 'spect, eh?"

Seikh bristled. "What do you mean by *that*?"

"You should know by now, Seikh, that the Scientians are the thinkers—not very good ones, but thinkers, nonetheless. You basically said it yourself just a few minutes ago. The Transmutants, on the other hand, they merely *feel*. They don't think. I don't know if they really know how to. Of course, the Scientians put a little too much emphasis on their thinking." Elihu kept tromping forward. "What exactly were you thinking about anyway, my son?"

Seikh hesitated, unsure if he should let Elihu know about his dream. He didn't want him to think that he was a Dreamer just like him, although Elihu seemed to think this already.

"You had a dream, didn't you, eh?" said Elihu, maintaining his forward march down the path but now with a slight limp from fatigue.

Unsettled, Seikh inquired, "How did you know that?"

"Like I said before, there are many things that have been revealed to me. But let me ask you this: It's a rather odd thing to have a dream, don't you think? Not many dreams around these days in Kosmon, what with them viewed as being irrational and all."

Seikh had caught up with Elihu and was now walking beside him. He had a musty, dirty scent.

"Tell me. What kind of dream did you have?"

"Nothing you would be interested in," Seikh replied in a disparaging tone.

"Oh, don't be so sure, my son. We Dreamers are very interested in dreams. Why do you think they call us 'Dreamers,' eh? We are mocked as dreamers, you know. I long, however, for the day to be called by what we really are: Seers." He seemed to let his mind ponder on days past. "We Seers once dreamed some of the most interesting dreams. At times, some of the dreams were actually real."

"Real?"

"Yes, yes. Quite real. Not really dreams at all."

Seikh silently held onto the words "quite real" for the next hour or so. He could hear Elihu breathing deeply. Seikh had taken his place again behind Elihu as they trudged down the dark path. Only the glow of the torch lit the way. Seikh kept thinking about the dream and how real it had felt. He pondered all that had occurred until now and mulled over all the questions he wanted to ask Elihu. He was unsure whether to ask them or not, but his curious nature eventually got the best of him when he muttered, "Mine was real."

"*What* was real?" The long silence had evidently caused Elihu to miss the connection with their previous conversation an hour ago.

"My dream. I could even smell things."

Elihu stopped abruptly and Seikh almost ran into him.

Elihu turned and began interrogating Seikh. "Smell things, you say? What else could you do in this dream? Did you hear things? See things?"

"Well, yes. There was a table and creatures sitting around it. They were eating. There were all kinds of food, and it was very pleasing to the eyes."

"What kind of creatures? Did they say anything or do anything?" Elihu was very persistent and excited.

"They didn't say much to me directly at first. I sat there for what seemed like forever. But then one of them asked me to join them."

"Did you?" Elihu asked anxiously.

"Uh, well, yes. I couldn't help myself. The food was very good, and we talked about the strangest of things. Their stories were of a world I never heard of. It was all very interesting, and we became quite good friends, so much so I didn't want to leave."

As he recalled the entire dream to Elihu, Seikh felt as if he was reliving it. It had been one of the most wonderful experiences he ever had. It brought a sense of satisfaction to his soul as he recounted every detail to Elihu. But now it seemed like such a long time ago and so far away, although it had occurred the night before.

When Seikh told him of the creature who appeared very bright and how his platter of meat seemed to have turned the whole course of events, Elihu appeared even more interested. After a moment of contemplation,

Elihu spoke, "Tell me: Did you ever hear a voice speak, a low and calm voice?"

"I heard the creature with the platter speak like that."

"Hmm." Elihu went back to thinking. His eyes bounced back and forth.

"What is it?"

Elihu responded, but ignored the question. "Did you hear the voice again at any time?"

"Come to think of it," said Seikh as he pondered, "at the end of the dream, I did. And I think it may have been the same voice that led me here to you."

"Led you here to me?" interrupted Elihu. "A voice did that?"

"Yeah. It was really odd. It would tell me where to go and how to turn, and I ran through some type of space-time tunnel. But if I didn't follow the voice's instructions the tunnel would just disappear . . ."

Elihu's eyes widened. "Oh, Seikh. Do you know what this means? That was no dream you had. You had a vision!"

Seikh was flummoxed. He had never heard of a vision. "A vision?"

"Yes. The Speech gave you a vision. It's the way he communicates. It's like a dream, except it's real."

"*Who* communicates?" asked Seikh.

"The Speech! Don't tell me you don't know about The Speech, my boy!"

"I can't say that I do."

Elihu began fumbling with his staff and pacing back and forth. Mumbling, he appeared to be struggling to find the right words to say. "My, my," he said repeatedly. He whispered some things and then said, "Yes, it is true then." He finally stopped and looked at Seikh. "The Speech has indeed brought you to me. You are the one The Speech spoke of! I knew I wasn't going crazy in my old age." He began to laugh.

"But what are you—?"

"Shh!" interrupted Elihu. It was quiet in the cave except for a distant sound of horse hooves.

"What is that?" Seikh whispered.

"My guess is that it's the ones looking for you. I hear the hooves of horses, and only Surek's men have horses."

"But Surek is the Sultan of Kosmon. Why would he be looking for me, and how would he know I am here?"

"Surek and his men—if you can call them that—were here last night. They came here and rounded up all the Seers."

Seikh was perplexed.

"The *Dreamers*," responded Elihu.

Seikh nodded. "They know where you live?" Seikh asked indignantly. He couldn't believe it. "Then why did you lead us back here?" Seikh's emotions were aroused. "I knew it! You have led me down here so that I might be captured and destroyed!"

"Settle down, son, and stop acting like a Transmutant! So foolish! I did not lead you here; The Speech did. And someone must have been keeping watch over the cave and then reported that they saw you enter. And have you forgotten that I told you that this path leads beyond the home of the Seers into the Woods of Ivory? Stop your fuming and follow me. I will lead you to safety in the woods."

For a few moments, Seikh did not move. Elihu looked at him gravely.

"Are you going to trust me, or not?"

Seikh nodded.

4

Petra

E lihu pulled Seikh by the arm as they walked swiftly down the Path of Sedeq.

"Come on! Quick lagging behind!" puffed Elihu.

For an old Dreamer, thought Seikh, *he can move rather quickly.* "They won't be able to catch up to us, will they?" Seikh asked.

"Not anytime soon," Elihu responded, gasping for breath. "They are on horses. They will either leave them behind because of the narrowness of the cave or they will have to take it slowly. Either way, we have time on our side. But if we want a meal for strength, then we must still hurry. We will stop by my place for food before going to the Woods."

They continued descending down the path for at least another half hour, winding back and forth. They came to what seemed like a long hall that led down a hill. The walls were tight, and the ceiling was low. Seikh felt like he was going to fall down the steep hill just as Elihu grabbed Seikh.

"Whoa! Stop!"

Right before them the path abruptly ended, and darkness surrounded them. Even the light from Elihu's torch no longer illuminated the walls of the cave. Seikh sensed that they had come out the other end of the hall.

"Be careful here. Wait until I light it up," Elihu commented while slowly moving forward.

"Light what up? I can't see anything." Seikh didn't even know whether the hall was still behind him or if they had made another turn.

Elihu reached out the torch as if to light something. Slowly, a line of fire began to appear, becoming longer and growing along what looked like a rocky wall. The line of fire made its way around the perimeter of the wall, but soon began branching downward and in all directions, lighting what looked like small troughs lining stone streets and roofs of small dwellings below. As the place became increasingly illuminated, Seikh noticed he was standing in a very large, oval-shaped room as large as a small city. The dome-shaped ceiling of the cave stood at least one thousand feet high, and the room stretched at least a mile in one direction and three quarters of a mile in the other. Once the small city was entirely lit, Seikh observed that he was standing at the top of a very large stone stairway that led down into the city made of stone dwellings. He stood gazing at the city emanating a golden glow.

"Welcome to the City of Petra," Elihu trumpeted.

"This is amazing!" responded Seikh in awe. "The Dreamers have lived here for three hundred years—in this underground city made of rock?"

He scanned the city from one end to the other. It was a marvelous work of masonry, but Seikh noticed broken jars and furniture, and carts strewn about the narrow stone streets. Many doors and windows were splintered and broken. Toppled food baskets littered the streets. Even many of the walls on the dwellings looked tarnished in black. The city looked like it had been pillaged.

Seikh turned somberly to Elihu. "What happened here? And where are the Dreamers?"

"The burning of the Dreamers at the stake last evening was the last of them. Laying siege to this city was the first act of violence against them in years. Surek and his army came here last night, armed with bows and javelins, and proclaimed that the judgment of the Dreamers had finally come. The Dreamers attempted to flee by the Path of Sedeq that continues on the far end of the city and leads to the Woods of Ivory. Surek and his men ran through the streets after them, killing any who resisted. Those who did not resist were bound, taken out of the city, placed in wooden carts, and taken to the Hinnom Meadow." Elihu paused and then spoke gravely, "You know the rest. Fortunately, a few of the Dreamers escaped. I presume they made it to the Woods of Ivory."

"How did you escape?" Seikh inquired.

"Thankfully, my dwelling is on the far end of the city where the Path of Sedeq continues. But while I was one of the fortunate ones who escaped, I did not do so unscathed. I was helping the Dreamers reach the path on the other side. There were women and children. Arrows and javelins were flying all around me. Some of the Dreamers were struck right in front of me. As the last ones reached the path, several Dreamers and I moved the stone in front of the opening to close it off so Surek's men could not reach us. I am very glad we thought years ago of a stone door to close that path off in case of an emergency."

Elihu's account gave Seikh chills. He tried to imagine the chaos and the blood spilled—Dreamers running through the stone streets to save their lives. It was difficult to fathom a battle happening just last night while he was soundly sleeping and having his vision, to imagine any of what Elihu said to be true. One thought led to another, and Seikh found himself believing he caught a discrepancy in Elihu's story.

"If you escaped with some of the Dreamers, how did you get back up to the mouth of the cave? And *why* would you want to come back?"

"I will tell you more, Seikh," replied Elihu, "as we make our way across the city. But we must get going. I'm sure Surek and his men are still making their way, and we must eat at my house before continuing on to the Woods."

Elihu and Seikh descended the large stone steps into the city. Seikh guessed there must have been one hundred steps before they reached the street below. As they entered the city and saw the carnage, the battle from the night before became more real to Seikh. Splintered wood, smashed fruit, pot shards, arrows, and javelins littered the streets. He even detected a scent of charred wood in the air. The doors to the dwellings were all open. Seikh imagined how no one would have given a thought to closing them as they ran for their lives.

As Elihu pressed on through the streets, Seikh found himself surveying as much of the city as possible. He still marveled at how an entire city made from stone was underground. People had been living in stone dwellings and yet he had never heard of it. No story about it had ever been told to him and there was no record of it in the Annals of Kosmon, the books he learned from at school. The secret stone city had been kept from him. He wondered if anyone else in Kosmon had heard of the city.

Did Surek and his men know about the city before last night? If they knew, did anyone else? Why would the city be kept secret from me?

"Another fifteen minutes and we shall be there," said Elihu as he followed the street to the right as it wound around what looked like a marketplace. Just behind the market Seikh saw a body of water flowing gently, perhaps several feet deep.

"Is that a river?"

"You could say that," replied Elihu. "It's a canal that we Seers carved into the floor. It runs all the way back to where we started, just slightly to the left and outside the cave. It is fed by the river you crossed where you entered. It has provided us water all these years, and it's our only source of water for the city. Further to the west we actually made several distributaries where it splits and feeds into the rest of the city."

"All of you Dreamers really lived here?" Seikh asked.

Elihu stopped and turned. Seikh halted just before running into him. Elihu looked flabbergasted. "Seers! We are the Seers! And what in the world do they teach you these days?"

"I mean," stumbled Seikh, "I have never heard of this city, and yet it is amazingly built for people to actually live here. It's like a secret city waiting to be unearthed, like a lost city made up in books. It's just surreal."

"You aren't dreaming this time, boy, eh? This city is as real as you are." Elihu pinched Seikh's arm. "Surely you have enough actual rational thought in that brain of yours to realize when to trust your senses, eh?" Elihu turned and continued down the street. "It seems to me that there may be many things you have not been told. Perhaps your schoolbooks, the Annals of Kosmon, have left a few things out."

Seikh grabbed Elihu by the arm. "Why? Why is it that I have not been told so many things? First, I find out that Mother and Father may not really be my parents, and now this city—"

"Seikh, my son. You will find that the best way—not necessarily the right way, mind you—to get someone to do or believe something is by not telling them everything, to keep secrets. To withhold information, or have only one voice speak, is sometimes a means to control you, to twist your will." Elihu's gaze seemed to penetrate into Seikh's mind. "Let us keep going. Just around the next bend we will be at my dwelling, and we shall eat."

Elihu led Seikh down a long, narrow, stone road that curved slightly to the left. As they walked, Seikh noticed a ten-foot-tall wall topped by a walkway lining the right side of the stone street.

"Does that walkway go around the entire city?"

"Yes," answered Elihu. "We built it so we could walk from one end of the city to the other more quickly. When the Seers lived here . . ." Elihu's words trailed off solemnly, as if to memorialize them. "It could get quite crowded in the streets. It was helpful while we lived here, but ultimately it was our undoing. Surek and his men used it to surround us."

Seikh glanced up at the wall. Blood stained it, and the remains of arrows and javelins hung over the top. No remains of the dead Dreamers were visible—no clothes, weapons, or bodies. He did not give much thought to this oddity but continued his survey of the stone street and the stone dwellings to his left. More bloodstains sprinkled the street than anywhere else in the city. The bulk of the battle must have taken place here. Seikh thought of the families, especially the children, who must have suffered greatly.

How could the calm, rational Scientians have done such a thing?

"Did they kill the children?" asked Seikh.

Elihu turned and replied, "They killed *all* of the Seers—slaughtered them in cold blood while their cries resounded throughout the city, making all of us tremble with fear, pain, and tears."

"But how could they? They were just children. Why? Who were they going to hurt?" Seikh asked, horrified.

"To Scientians and Transmutants they weren't children. They weren't even persons to them. They were nothing but *germs* of life that would one day become a threat to them. When the Scientians came here last night, they were intent on exterminating all the Seers to ensure that the Ancient Order would never rise again. And if the children of the Seers had been left alive, a continued threat of the Ancient Order would remain." He paused and looked at the ground. His eyes were dim and his posture low. He looked as if he had just been beaten in the worst of wars. "The Ancient Order," he continued, his voice lifting higher, "was a time of peace. There was no violence, no sickness, and certainly no plague. Kosmon was a sanctuary. All peoples loved one another."

"Even the Scientians and Dreamers?"

"*Seers*, my boy!" yelled Elihu, bumping his staff on Seikh's head. "There were no Scientians or Seers at that time—and no Transmutants either. There was only one race: the Ancients. These other races of creatures—the Scientians and all—came about by the plague. The plague changed everyone and *everything*, just as your vision revealed to you about the creatures who surrounded the table and ate the meat. There is a cure to all this madness, this plague that dominates Kosmon, and the Scientians have attempted to find it for thousands of years. But they haven't been able to, and they won't be able to either."

"And why not?" Seikh asked indignantly, perturbed by Elihu's lack of faith in the intellectual powers of the Scientians.

"Because the very cure they are looking for is the very thing they have rejected. And the Scientians and the Transmutants are now in league with the one who introduced the plague—Abaddon, the Ruler of Kosmon." Elihu's eyes fixed upon Seikh, and his grave voice produced shivers down Seikh's spine. "But you, Seikh, have been chosen to find the cure and defeat Abaddon."

Elihu came a little closer to Seikh and looked deeply into his eyes. Seikh was confused and he shook at the mysteries Elihu was revealing. *What do I know about the plague? And who is this Ruler Abaddon?* It all sounded preposterous.

"Yes," continued Elihu, "*you* are to find the cure, Seikh, and loose the grip that Abaddon has upon Kosmon, to set it free, to bring healing to all. That's what this is all about. Don't you see? The Speech has brought you here, and I am leading you to where you need to go next to find the cure. Kosmon must be saved, and you have been chosen."

"What!?" yelled Seikh. "Chosen? You are out of your mind, you old fool!"

Elihu threw his staff down in disgust and stepped close to Seikh, grabbing and shaking him by the arms, speaking in the most commanding voice, "Listen to me, Seikh!"

Suddenly, a gale of wind began to blow, and in the wind Seikh heard the voice from his vision and his travel through the Woods of Ebony. It was low and calm, yet loud enough to hear over the wind.

"Listen to Elihu. He guides you."

The voice trailed off, along with the wind, until quietness was restored in the city.

"What was that?" Seikh whispered, trembling and not knowing what to expect next.

"It was The Speech." Elihu let go of Seikh. He then spoke with the utmost seriousness. "Listen to me, Seikh. You must follow my guidance as The Speech has spoken. There isn't much time. Surek and his men will be here soon. I must get you to safety and send you on the path that you must travel to find the cure for Kosmon and destroy Abaddon. I do not know the cure myself, but I know where to find it, and The Speech has chosen you to go there."

"But why me? And why doesn't he just tell me himself what to do and how to get there? Why all this confusion?" Seikh was greatly distressed. "I don't understand." Seikh began sobbing. He rubbed his hands through the dark brown hair with gray streaks atop his head. "I don't know who you really are. I don't know who to trust. Everything I have ever known has been taken from me—Mother, Father. Everything I thought I knew seems to be wrong." Seikh collapsed to the ground and buried his face in his hands. "What is this Speech? What am I to do, and where am I to go? Who should I listen to?" Seikh sat on the cold stone street, gasping and sobbing.

Just then, a still, small voice spoke throughout the city. "Peace. Be still."

Elihu bent down and laid his hands on Seikh's head. "Yes, peace. Be still," Elihu said softly.

He then picked up his staff and lifted Seikh to his feet and put him over his shoulders. He carried Seikh down the road until they reached a very small, solitary stone house.

5

Surek

E lihu set Seikh down at the front door of his house. "We are here," Elihu commented as he unlocked the door. "Let us talk while we eat."

Seikh, now calm, followed Elihu inside. It was dark and cool. Elihu struck a match and lit several oil lamps. As the light filled the house, Seikh noticed it was only one room, and it was round and had no windows. To the left was a short, round table, and on the opposite side of the room a small, short cot sat nestled against the wall. Directly before him against the wall were a few cupboards and what looked like a washbasin. Elihu was already swiftly putting together a small meal, swiping bread from the cupboards and pouring drinks from a pitcher. As Seikh curiously watched Elihu scurry about, he noticed something strange on the floor. It wasn't very large, yet it was long and narrow.

"What is that?" Seikh inquired, pointing at the floor.

"Why that's a door."

Elihu looked at Seikh and smirked before calling him over to the table that was now set for a meal. They both sat on the floor, reclining.

"That is my secret trap-door. Inside is a tunnel that leads all the way to the Woods of Ebony. That's how I escaped Surek and his men when they came last night. After I helped the other Seers escape on the Path of Sedeq by closing the tunnel with the stone door, I quickly ran into my house and descended into the secret passage. I pulled this table and that rug on the bed over to cover the secret door." He paused. "It worked, eh? I'm still alive!" He smiled.

Seikh listened intently, grinning a bit from Elihu's attempt to be funny.

"Here have some drink, bread, and meat," Elihu said. "This will give us the strength we need for our journey. We haven't much time now, so we must eat quickly." Elihu placed bread and meat in front of Seikh, and then said, "To the great Speech, the one who guides, instructs, and governs our thoughts and actions!" He paused, looking at Seikh as if waiting for a reply.

Slowly, softly, and with little confidence, Seikh replied, "Yes. To The Speech."

"Hmm. You truly know nothing of The Speech, do you?"

"I can't say I do, sir. At least not much if I do."

"The Speech is the one who saved you from the mob last night and directed you here to me. He is the rightful Ruler of Kosmon, although Abaddon, the Ruler of the Shadows, believes he is. The Speech is known by his words. He speaks to whom he chooses, and he guides and directs those who listen and obey his words."

"What does he look like?" asked Seikh.

"No, no, no," Elihu replied quickly while stuffing bread into his mouth. "He can't be seen. He's *unseen*."

"Unseen? Well, can we touch him, taste him, smell him?" Seikh inquired.

"None of those. Only hear."

Seikh sipped from his cup, then slammed it down on the table in disgust. "If you cannot see, touch, taste, or smell him, and you can only hear him, then how do you know he exists and that what you hear is this 'Speech?' How can you put such trust in this 'Speech?' This sounds an awful lot like the mythology I was warned to stay away from."

"Let me ask you a question, dear boy: What do you learn in school? Do you learn arithmetic? Do you learn the sciences?"

Elihu continued to eat.

"Yes, of course," replied Seikh. "The Annals of Kosmon are filled with numerous lessons in these studies."

"Does the number one exist?"

"Why of course!"

"How do you know?"

"Because I can see it! I write it down and there it is right in front of me."

Elihu stopped eating and looked at Seikh, "And what if I erase it?"

Seikh sat quietly, puzzled.

"Does the number one no longer exist?" Elihu asked.

"I suppose," began Seikh hesitantly, "it still exists for I can still think of the number one."

"And note," remarked Elihu, beginning to eat again, "that the number one cannot be touched. You can't smell it, and you certainly cannot hear it! But yet it still exists! My, my. How mysterious, eh?" Elihu chuckled a bit. "So, tell me, young Seikh: Did you hear The Speech?"

"Well, I heard *something*."

"And more than once?"

"Yes."

"Then why doubt the existence of The Speech, especially when I too have heard the exact same voice? I testify to this, I tell you." Elihu gulped the final swig of his drink, put down the cup, and sighed, "Ahh! You see, my boy. You have more evidence that The Speech exists than the number one, not to mention *all* the numbers, eh? You can at least hear The Speech! The number one is technically just inside your head!" He poked Seikh in the forehead. "Besides, I've heard him more than you have and for a lot longer, so I know who he is and what his plans are. Well, at least some of them."

Seikh was becoming more convinced by Elihu's words. His reasoning made sense. He had heard The Speech, and he had spoken in the cave along the road to both Elihu and him. There didn't seem to be any good reason to question that this was indeed a fact. "So, what are The Speech's plans?" asked Seikh.

By now Elihu was cleaning up the table. "That's where you come in. Ever since the Scientian War, the plague of Kosmon has grown worse. People have become more violent and evil as Abaddon continues to cast his shadow over Kosmon and its people. The Woods of Ebony were once a part of the Woods of Ivory—light and filled with peace. But now Abaddon's shadow has engulfed the Woods for so long that it has become black as the night. Even the Kosmonians themselves have come under Abaddon's rule. Some of the Scientians are beginning to change into creatures just like the Transmutants. That's what the plague does—it changes the very nature of who you are. These are signs that the final battle is drawing nearer: the battle between The Speech and Abaddon, the one who brought the plague into Kosmon to destroy and conquer it for his own."

Elihu was now speaking with intensity. Seikh noticed that the light from the lamps was dimming inside the cool stone house. Elihu was sitting on the small bed and Seikh was still comfortable reclining at the table. Elihu stood up and continued his story.

"After the Scientian War, The Speech spoke one last time before being silent for nearly three hundred years. He gave a prophecy. He told the Seers not to be frightened that Surek and the Scientians had won the war. He said not to fear that they will be used as instruments by Abaddon, but that one day a Seer would rise, one born of a Scientian. He would seek and find the one person who has the cure for the plague: the great Ancient One, Lamlorde. And when the time was right, The Speech would call this young Seer to find him."

Elihu's words slowly flowed from his mouth. He looked at Seikh and immediately Seikh understood that he was talking about him.

"I can't be that Seer!" protested Seikh. "I'm a Scientian, like my father! I'm no Seer!"

"No, Seikh. I was there when you were born to your mother, Lucy, and your father, Dr. Ichabod. When you were born you had the clear features of a Seer. Your parents feared for your life and so to protect you they told others you had wandered off from the Seers and that they decided to adopt you. They convinced the Scientians to let you live among the Kosmonians and that they would train you in the Annals of Kosmon so you wouldn't be a threat to them. I see they have done a decent job teaching you the Kosmonian ways—you have lost a lot of your Seerean features. You have evolved into more of a Scientian than a Seer."

Seikh eyes scanned the room frantically. "No! This can't be true!" he yelled. "Why didn't Mother and Father tell me? This is a lie!"

"But it isn't, Seikh! You can see for yourself that you have hair like a Scientian, but you also have white hair like me. And your arms and legs are like mine. Haven't you ever wondered why you look different from your father and mother and the other Kosmonians? Haven't you ever wondered why everyone looked at you differently? It's no coincidence that you are named Seikh."

Seikh's eyes widened. The truth hit him. He knew it was true. "That's why they wanted to kill me last night, too. Because I am a Dreamer just like you. It makes sense now—my dreams and my appearance." Seikh began stroking the hair on his head and arms. Confused, he asked, "Elihu, what should I do? Surek will certainly kill me if he finds me, for I am a Seer!"

"Yes, Surek will kill you if he finds you. He will do this because Abaddon's shadow covers him. He is Abaddon's pawn. To escape his clutches, you must listen and obey The Speech! You have been chosen to find Lamlorde, the one who holds the cure which will destroy Abaddon's grip on Kosmon, lifting the shadows of evil that plague it. You must trust The Speech, my son. And he will even lift the shadows of Abaddon from you."

"Lamlorde? Is he real?" Seikh asked incredulously.

"Yes, he is as real as I am standing here before you. But he must be found. He has been gone for thousands of years. He is the only one who has the cure."

Elihu and Seikh were now standing face-to-face in the middle of the stone hut. Elihu's hands were on Seikh's shoulders. Only one lamp remained lit, but Elihu appeared as a light in the room. The hair on his head and face shone with brilliance. His clothes appeared to gleam. His eyes were like warm, golden lamps. There was something about Elihu that made Seikh desire now to be like him. Everything Elihu had told Seikh seemed to him as true. He began to feel as if a weight was being lifted from his shoulders. His thoughts were clearer than ever, as if light had begun to fill his mind. A sense of peace came upon him. Oddly, he felt like he was growing taller and that his physical features were changing. Yes! He *was* changing. He could now see directly into Elihu's eyes! He felt an unfamiliar calmness was over him, as if he could conquer Kosmon all by himself and live forever.

Seikh stared into Elihu's eyes. Slowly and softly he spoke, "I will trust The Speech."

With a smile, Elihu responded, "Then he will protect you from the shadow of Abaddon."

Without warning, the final lamp went out. It was completely dark. A shout was heard in the stone city. "I have fooound yooou and now you will die."

The voice was like a hissing snake. It was low and made Seikh shudder with fear.

"It's Surek! How did he get here so fast?" Elihu said as he lit another lamp and handed it to Seikh. Elihu opened the secret door in the floor. "Quickly! Hop in! You must hide in here."

"But how will we get to the Woods of Ivory? Can't we just escape on the Path of Sedeq?"

"No. It is too late for that now. There's no time to move the stone door away from the tunnel entrance. You must hide in here." Elihu paused and Seikh could tell he was thinking. "No, no. Forget hiding. You must take this tunnel to the Woods of Ivory."

"Wait! What about you?"

"I will distract Surek so you can escape, eh?" Elihu said, smirking, proud of his deceitful plan. "Make sure to take the hidden passage to the right. The one on the left will lead you back into the City of Petra and into the hand of Surek. Now go!"

Seikh jumped through the secret door and into the passage. Right behind him, Elihu swiftly closed the door. He could hear Elihu pulling the rug over it and then the table. As Seikh looked around in the passage, he could see nothing but a small tunnel to the right and to the left. The tunnels were so small that he would have to crawl. As he prepared to begin his escape, he could hear the galloping of horses' hooves and voices echoing from the cave. Seikh paused and listened. Instead of turning right as Elihu directed, he scurried to the left. *There's more than one way to find out what's going on.*

He placed the handle of the lamp in his mouth and began crawling through the small tunnel. As he went along the voices grew louder, as he drew nearer to Surek and his men.

After about a hundred yards, he came upon another door. He put down the lamp and, sitting on his knees, he nudged the door open. Through the crack, he could see he was in another stone house, just like Elihu's. The secret door was positioned just right so Seikh could see out the front door of the house and into the city streets.

As Seikh peered through the crack, he saw someone standing on the roof of the stone house across the street. It was Elihu, with his back toward him. Just beyond Elihu, on top of another house, was a hooded figure clothed from head to foot in black, sitting on a black horse, facing Elihu. Beside him stood two red horses, both saddled by what looked like Transmutants. They, however, looked more horrific than any Transmutant Seikh had ever seen. Their faces were a mix between a Scientian and a snake. They were mostly covered with brown hair but had black scales peeking through. They had snake eyes and forked tongues that would occasionally slither out of their mouths. They, too, were wearing black. All around Elihu stood more black horses saddled with the threatening figures.

"Weee have fooound you, O ancient onnne," hissed the figure in black.

Elihu cried out, "O, Surek! I can see that Abaddon's shadow has been cast completely over you. You are as dark as the night, eh? What have you come here for? For me? I am of little harm to you. I am an old Seer and in no condition to be of any threat to Kosmon."

"You can ssstop with your ancient sussspicions about shadowy figuresss. There isss no one who controlsss me except mysssself. And I do not come here for yoooou," he hissed, "I ssseek the Ssseeker. My men sssaw him enter your city and ssspeaking with you."

"I do not know what you speak of, O Sultan of Kosmon. No Scientian boy would want to come here—to a place of bloodshed and death."

"Ah, ha! Yesss. Your friendsss seemed to have had a little missshap last night, I sssee."

"Don't act surprised," replied Elihu. "You and your men are the ones who left this city in the shadow of death."

"And I sssee that *you* essscaped. How fortunate to have you and the boy. Two for the price of one."

"There is no boy here, I tell you."

"Perhapsss my men can help yoooou remember where he isss." A long forked tongue emerged from the hood as he said these last words. Surek's men closed in on Elihu.

It had been weeks since Seikh had seen Surek. At that time, he was like any other Scientian. He had stopped by his house to visit his father. But now Surek appeared as some horrid creature, wearing black. This was not the Sultan of Kosmon he had known. Surek had been over to his house with Mother and Father quite often throughout his youth in the little log house in the Woods of Ebony. He was a rational, calm, clear-thinking Scientian who just wanted to find the cure for the plague. He and Father had worked together. But now Surek had changed. He was something terrifying.

"Oh Surek," Elihu began as he addressed Surek once again. "Isn't it a cure for the plague that you seek rather than the life of some boy or myself? Isn't this your true goal? Why worry about some young boy who can do nothing and has nothing to do with what you seek?"

"Ssso, you have ssseen him, haven't you?" Surek's horse neighed with anxiety and turned slightly to the right. "And what I truuuly sseek, my dear ancient fool, isss to bring an end to thossse who desssire to put an end to Kosssmon. It wasss promisssed that thisss young boy, SSeikh, would be taught to put off the mythsss of the Dreamersss and that he would not be a threat to civilizzzation. But yoooou have been sssecretly indoctrinating him."

"No, no. That is not true. I have done nothing of the sort!" Elihu said.

"It is not in the nature of a Dreamer to lie, isss it? Here you ssstand condemned by your own wordsss, for it hasss been told to me that you first ssspoke with him not many yearsss ago in the Woods of Ebony near hisss housse. And you have been in contact with him ever since!"

"There is a difference, O Surek, between speaking and overseeing. I only watched over the boy to make sure that no harm came to him, but I never spoke to him."

"I am not here to argue over wordsss, Elihu. You know where he isss, and you mussst be dessstroyed along with him to save Kosssmon! The foolish fairy talesss of the Ancient Order will never rule again! Bind him!"

Surek's low voice bellowed throughout the cave. Some of his men drew forward and grabbed a hold of Elihu and began to bind him.

"Surek!" Elihu screamed while his staff hit the ground and he struggled to remain free, "Kosmonian law forbids the death of anyone without a trial."

"Kosssmonian law?" Surek snickered. "There isss no law in Kosssmon besssides me. *I* am the law."

Elihu wriggled out of the grasp of Surek's men and fell down the curved rooftop of the stone house and hit the street. He struggled to get up, for his hands were tied behind his back. Surek waved his men to back away from Elihu. Surek then stretched out his hands as if he was going to shoot Elihu with a bow and arrow. Instantly a bow and arrow appeared, glowing red. "Now you will die!" shouted Surek.

"Come quickly Lamlorde! Come quickly!" said Elihu, closing his eyes.

Surek released the glowing red arrow from his bow. It flew through the air straight and swiftly. It penetrated through Elihu's chest and made a small thundering noise and disappeared, leaving a deep wound. Elihu fell to the ground. He rolled over and was now facing Seikh as he peeked through the secret door in the floor of the stone house. Elihu caught a glimpse of him and mouthed, "Seikh! Find Lamlorde. Listen to The Speech."

He laid his head down on the cold stone street. He was dead.

6

Abaddon

Seikh sat speechless in the secret passage, still looking through the crack of the secret door. The ground began to shake and rumble. He could hear dishes falling and doors rattling as the earthquake jostled the city. The horses on which Surek and his men were riding became frightened and began kicking and neighing furiously. Many of them fell to the ground. Then a large thunderclap resounded throughout the city. As Seikh's eyes rested upon Elihu's lifeless figure, a gale of wind rushed through the street. Elihu's body appeared to turn to dust, and a whirlwind carried it up into the air and disappeared.

Within seconds everything was quiet like before. Surek spoke to his men, "Get up! Elihu isss gone! Now find the boy! He isss hiding in the city!" Immediately Surek's men mounted their horses and began trotting through the streets, with the two red horses in the lead.

Seikh fell back into the secret passage. The door closed with a small thud. Putting the lamp's handle in his mouth, he began crawling as fast as he could back to Elihu's house. He quickly passed by the secret door leading into Elihu's house and then found himself going through the part of the passage which Elihu had told him to go initially. The passage was just large enough for him to raise his head. He crawled up and then down, to the right and to the left. His knees began to ache from grinding them on the hard stone. The palms of his hands became mixed with sweat and chalk from rock dust on the floor. It was dark and he could see only as far as the light of the lamp would allow him. The voices of Surek's men and the clopping of horses' hooves echoed through the tunnel. Seikh could not tell where they were, and he became scared they would catch him. The voices sounded like they were getting closer.

I must go faster.

Just as the tunnel curved to the right, he heard a quiet whisper: "Seikh!"

He stopped. He stretched out flat in the tunnel and looked behind him.

He heard the whisper again: "Seikh!"

"Who's there?"

"You don't have to run. You can come back home," said the whispering voice, drawing out its words.

The voice didn't sound like Surek's.

"Who are you?" asked Seikh. "And what do you want? I can't see you. Show yourself."

"I am your protector, and I can help you find what you are looking for. I can give you peace and understanding."

"Are you The Speech? Where are you? Show yourself!" Seikh said.

He looked furiously up and down the tunnel. He saw nothing, but he could sense a presence. He got back on his knees frantically and began crawling, but he lost his grip of the lamp and it fell. As he stretched out his hand to grasp it, in front of him an eerie shadow appeared in the tunnel. It hovered just above the floor and was stretched out as if lying down. Its shadowy, hooded head peered at Seikh's face.

"Think more clearly, Seikh," said the voice. "What are you doing in this tunnel? You need to go back and help the Scientians find the cure for what plagues Kosmon. They have nearly found it, and all they need is your help. You hold the key that will finally unlock the mystery of the cure. You can ring in the new Kosmon—the peaceful Eschatolis—a Kosmon without violence and the plague. Keep the shackles of the ancient myths from binding you."

"What?" Seikh questioned anxiously. "Are you The Speech? I must listen only to him!"

"Yes. I am a Speech, and I will heal you," said the shadow. "Your hands and knees are worn, and you are tired and weary. I will give you rest."

Seikh looked at his knees. His pants were ripped and stained with blood. Through the excitement he had not felt them become scraped from crawling. His left knee was covered in blood from a gash, and now he noticed how much his knees were throbbing. He looked at his palms: the skin was peeling, and blood had already begun to crust over.

He looked back up at the shadow. It was floating silently, as if waiting for his response. Then, at once, the words of Elihu came to his mind: Abaddon, Ruler of the *Shadows*. This was Abaddon!

"No! You . . . you are Abaddon! You seek to destroy, not heal."

"To destroy or to heal is a matter of perspective. A knife in the hands of a physician heals. In the hands of a warrior, it destroys."

"Then you must be a warrior!" screamed Seikh, throwing the lamp at the shadow.

The shadow immediately flew at him and then disappeared as a sound of rushing wind blew through the tunnel. The lamp passed through the shadow and tumbled through the tunnel as if rolling down a hill and then made a crashing sound. A small faint light glimmered in the distance.

Seikh crawled slowly through the dark toward the light. He felt the tunnel descending. As he approached the light, the tunnel opened up into a large hallway and emptied out onto a floor about eight feet down. Seikh peered into the much larger passage. The light was coming from the lamp he had thrown. Luckily, it survived the tumble.

Seikh jumped down into the passage and tried to gather the pieces of the lamp, but it was no use. The glass was shattered beyond repair and the oil was quickly oozing out. The light was quickly fading. He looked around the much wider and taller passage, one that was large enough for him to stand in. Just above his head on the right was a torch protruding from the wall like a trumpet ready to be blown. Quickly he grabbed it, dabbed as much spilled oil from the ground as he could, and lit it. The torch erupted into a blazing fire. From the size of the flames, Seikh discerned that it must have already been doused with some kind of fuel. Perhaps it had been left by the Seers in case of an emergency. Seikh was thankful.

He stood in the long, tall passage. Surek and his men could no longer be heard. Only the constant dripping of water was audible. Exactly where it was coming from Seikh could not tell. It just quietly echoed down the hallway of stone.

Some water would be nice right about now.

He looked at his scraped knees and hands, desiring to clean them. Without further delay, he began his journey toward the Woods of Ivory through the secret tunnel.

It wasn't long before Seikh came upon the water he had heard dripping. On the right side of the passage water slowly seeped out of the wall, trickling to the floor, and gently flowing into a crack at the bottom of the opposite wall across the path. He placed the torch in a small hole in the wall, cupped his hands, and collected some water. He began cleaning his wounds. The water was cool and refreshing. He filled his hands with water and began lapping it up. He drank until he could drink no more and took a seat on the ground. He was tired and wanted to sleep. Drowsiness came over him like a thick fog and he fell asleep.

Within moments, Seikh found himself standing amid some woods on a dark, cold night. Light from a full moon was peering through the trees which stood as dark shadowy figures, giving a bluish hue throughout the woods.

"Seikh!" said a voice quietly. "Seikh!"

"Who are you?" Seikh replied.

"I am The Speech," the voice responded calmly. "The one who guides you."

"How do I know you are not Abaddon? There are so many voices! How do I know which one to listen to?"

"You will know me, Seikh, for I bring peace and life. Abaddon brings contradictions, strife, confusion, and destruction. And . . ." the voice paused. Seikh looked through the trees and a bright white light began filtering through the trees of the woods. "I bring light, dispelling the shadows!"

The light became brighter, and it began landing on the trees like snow, changing the trees and the ground into pure white. The night was turned into day, and the light became so bright it began to blind Seikh.

"Seikh!" came another voice. It was like the voice in the woods but something about it was different. "Seikh!" it cried out again but much louder.

Seikh opened his eyes. It had been a dream! He was sitting on the ground against the wall of the tunnel. But he heard the voice again. "Seikh!" He looked up and there again was the shadow he had seen before. Seikh grabbed the torch from the hole in the wall and began to run. He looked behind him and saw the shadow in hot pursuit, so he kept running as fast as he could.

The chase continued for what seemed like miles. The tunnel turned slightly to the left. A doorway lay just ahead in the bend, carved into the wall. It was sealed off with a large wooden door. On the right of it was a large, black, metal handle. Seikh ran toward it with all his strength. He stuck out his free hand and engaged the handle, turning it as swiftly as possible. It was unlocked!

He charged through the opening and slammed the door behind him. Gasping for breath, Seikh leaned against the door with the palm of his hands and his head bowed to the ground. He had outrun the shadow.

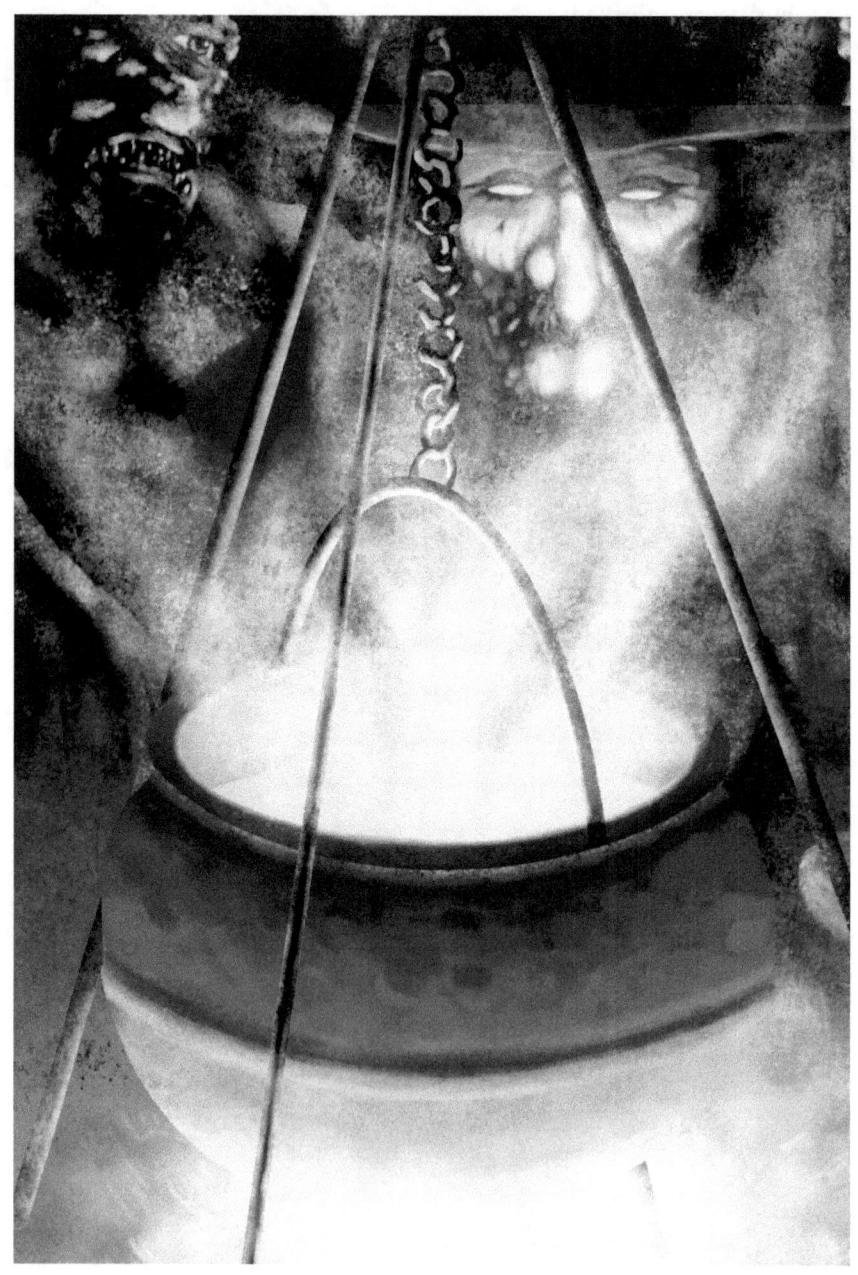

7

Sangoma

S eikh stood looking at the floor of the cave, trying to catch his breath, when he heard voices behind him. He slowly turned and found himself standing in a small room. In the center of the small corridor was a small fire with a large, black kettle strung up for cooking. Around the fire sat several figures. Seikh could see only their faces slightly glowing in the firelight. One figure stood out; it sat directly behind the kettle with its face just visible above the kettle's brim. It was a type of creature he had not seen before. It didn't look to be of the Scientian or Transmutant race, and neither did it look like a Dreamer. Dressed all in black, its face didn't have any hair on it, but it was covered in wrinkles and had a texture to it. A large, pointed nose protruded from underneath the black pointy hat upon its head. Seikh stared at the figure, and it spoke to him.

"I see you have finally made it." The voice was rather high and sounded much like a woman, and yet was cranky and old.

"Yes," Seikh replied, playing along.

The creature detected the hesitancy in his voice and began to question him. "You *are* the Informer, are you not?"

"Yes," replied Seikh without giving much thought to the question.

"What took you so long to get here? We've been waiting for a very long time," it said while looking him over with its glassy eyes. "We thought you'd never get here. We finally gave up and set up camp here."

"Well, I ran into a bit of trouble," Seikh replied, hoping he could think of something next to say.

"I can see that," it retorted quickly. "Your knees and legs look a little mangled."

The other figures around the fire chuckled in deep voices and repeated "mangled, yeah mangled." They all had bowls in front of them and were slurping up stew, perhaps drawn from the kettle sitting over the fire.

The figure spoke again, "Run into a pack of hungry gundigans? Those creatures can be quite ferocious when they smell a Scientian, you know." It didn't give him a second to answer, but continued. "So, did you capture that little Dreamer? Seikh, or whatever his name is?'"

"No, not exactly," Seikh replied hesitantly, hoping the creature would fill in the blanks of the story for him.

"Then where is he? You were supposed to lead him to us. Don't tell me you couldn't find him again after you reported to Surek that he entered the stone city?"

"Oh, no. It's not that." Seikh now realized that the Informer must have been the spy who reported to Surek that he had seen him enter the cave.

"Then what is it, O wise one?" screeched the creature sarcastically.

"Well," Seikh said, thinking as quickly as he could. "Surek decided to capture the Dreamer himself. He went down to the city of Petra with his men."

"Ah! I knew it!" it retorted in disgust. "Another adventure and capture spoiled!"

"And dinner!" yelled out the figures circling the fire.

"Calm down, you beasts! You will get your flesh as I promised—one way or another," the creature responded looking at them contemptuously. He turned back to Seikh. "If Surek wanted that Dreamer himself, why did he send us down here to wait on you to bring him to us?"

The other figures around the fire began to mumble and moan. Seikh had come closer to the fire and could see them more clearly. They were rather large creatures with scaley skin and one large eye in the middle of their heads. Their teeth glimmered in the dim light of the fire. Their teeth looked too small to be in their mouths and were spaced far apart. They all looked like large daffy monsters. Yet there was something very repulsive about them. Seikh had the feeling of uncleanness as he gazed upon them.

"Surek changed his plans once I reported that the Dreamer had entered the city," said Seikh. "He went to the city himself to destroy him and I went with him."

"Then why are you here now?" he asked, looking suspiciously at Seikh as if he wasn't sure whether to believe him.

"Once Surek was in the city," Seikh continued, "he found only a Dreamer named Elihu rather than the boy Dreamer, and then he told me to meet you and to let you know to return to his castle. That's why my knees are bloodied. I had to crawl from the city through the tunnel to get here."

The creature in the black pointy hat looked into Seikh's eyes. He hoped that the creature would believe his story.

"Tunnel? I do not know of any tunnel that leads from the city to here. What is this you are speaking of?" The creature looked more deeply into Seikh's eyes. He had made a misstep by mentioning the secret tunnel. "You do know who I am, don't you? I am Sangoma. I have been around for hundreds of years. You cannot trick me. If you are lying, I will find out and then you will pay with your life. These fellas," he said, looking at the monsters, "have an appetite for flesh. I would gladly feed you to them."

Sangoma slowly walked closer to the fire and took out a poker that had been lying there. The tip was glowing orange and red with heat. As he approached Seikh, he waved it in front of his face slowly, barely touching the hair of his face. "Slomo etchy proto myo," he said, and a light green fog formed in front of Seikh's face. The smell of it took his breath away. His senses began to dull, and his mind became numb. He felt like an empty shell and as if Sangoma was looking into his mind, discerning his thoughts and dividing them one from the other. Seikh could hear him speaking as if far away. "Hmm. Yes. I see that you are not who you say you are. But who? Who are you? You have some thoughts I cannot unlock. There is something protecting some of your thoughts." Seikh felt like he was in a dream. He could see the creature looking at him as if through the top of a barrel. The creature hummed and then was silent. It gasped and then let out a scream. "There is *light* in your thoughts!"

Seikh felt himself hit the ground. He awoke from his trancelike state, and he saw that Sangoma was now huddling near the monsters.

"No! You are not the Informer!" Sangoma was shrieking. "You have light in your thoughts! This is unheard of! A Scientian with light in his mind? *Who are you?*"

Seikh lay silently on the floor. He was limp and could not move. The monsters were visibly agitated and began to rise from around the fire. "Bind him up, you Pravitas!" Sangoma yelled. "I don't know where this light-minded fraud is from, but I know where he is going. To Surek!"

The monsters growled, hissed, and hollered as some of them walked a wooden cart with wobbly wheels from the far side of the room over to Seikh. Two monsters lifted Seikh off the ground like a toothpick and wrapped thick ropes around his body, tying his hands behind his back. The ropes were scratchy and coarse. They threw Seikh into the wooden cart like a rag doll, and in single file the monsters, with Sangoma in the lead, left the stone room dragging the cart with Seikh in it behind them.

Seikh awoke to the sound of the cart's ragged wooden wheels rolling over the stone floor of the tunnel. He had fallen asleep from the green fog Sangoma had entranced him with. As he struggled to gain consciousness, he noticed his head was covered with a dark sack with a hole just for his mouth and nose. He could not see anything. His body wobbled to and fro in the cart. The ropes dug into his wrists, hands, and the rest of his body. The hair of his legs, arms, and chest felt as if it were being slowly ripped from his skin. The monsters had wrapped him well.

As he lay there, he couldn't help but think about The Speech. This would be a great time for The Speech to help him escape.

Without The Speech and without Elihu, how will I ever begin to look for Lamlorde and get to the Woods of Ivory now?

He wished he had paid more attention when he was running down the hall of the cave and made the right turn. He wasn't sure if he had followed Elihu's directions or not.

As the cart swayed, Seikh barely overheard Sangoma speaking to the monsters.

"When we get to the exit of the tunnel, make sure to wrap this boy up as best you can. We don't want any hungry gundigans picking up his scent. We need to deliver him to Surek for questioning. We don't want him to be any gundigan's dinner, nor do we want any problems."

"But what about us?" asked one of the monsters just a little louder and more clearly. "Can't we have him for dinner?"

The other monsters chimed in, "Yeah, yeah! We're hungry!"

"No!" Sangoma screeched. "Aren't you listening to anything I'm saying, you dumb brutes? We have to take him to Surek!"

"Then what are we going to eat? You promised us flesh!" The monsters began to get rowdy, and the cart slowed and then stopped. Seikh felt hot and sweaty.

"Now, now. Just a minute! There's no reason to get so upset and surround me like you're going to roast me over a fire." Sangoma's voice was a little shaky and was now higher. "How about we go gundigan hunting? Hmm? You like gundigans, don't you? And! And!" His voice was playful and filled with anticipation. "If Surek doesn't want the boy, then you can play with him or eat him or whatever it is you Pravitas do."

"That sounds good, Sangoma!" said a monster. "What a good idea! Gundigans for a snack and the flesh for dinner!"

There was a brief silence and then another monster spoke up. "Wait a minute! Do you *promise*?"

"Yes. Of course! I promise," Sangoma replied.

"Okay, then. Gundigans now! Flesh later!"

The cart began to move again, rocking back and forth down the tunnel. The wheels were making an awful squealing noise. The squealing kept getting louder and then Seikh heard the sound of splintering wood. Crack! Without notice, the cart spilled Seikh onto the ground. The monsters began making a commotion and Sangoma yelled at them. "Quickly! Pick up the boy and leave the cart here!"

One of the monsters picked up Seikh, smashing his face into his hairy side. The dark sack that covered Seikh's face slid upward. The hole for the nose was now over his right eye and the hole for the mouth was over his nose. Seikh caught a glimpse of the wooden cart. It had entirely fallen apart. He moved his eyes to the left and right, but he couldn't see any of the monsters or Sangoma. He was faced behind them, being carried under one of the monster's arms.

The trip through the remainder of the tunnel was painful. The monster carrying Seikh gave little care to how he held him. For a while the monster hauled Seikh on his back, holding him by his ankles. Later, he shifted him and began dragging him by the feet. Then the monster curled him up around his neck and hung on to his head with one hand and his feet with the other. The flipping, flopping, bouncing, and dragging nauseated Seikh. Just when he thought he was about to get sick, Sangoma announced their arrival at the exit of the tunnel.

"Listen to me carefully!" All the monsters stopped. "Wrap the boy up. We're heading into the woods."

The monster who had a hold of Seikh rolled him in a large, thick, black blanket, leaving one of Seikh's eyes uncovered just enough so he could see. When they exited the tunnel, the monster picked up some straw and dead leaves from the ground and crammed it in between Seikh and the blanket. "There!" said the monster, looking over Seikh. "No gundigans should sniff you out now!" He chuckled as if quite proud of himself, and then stuffed him under his arm again, but this time with his face looking upward.

The monsters trudged forward, making their way across a river. Seikh reasoned it must be the same river that flowed in front of the mouth of the cave where he first saw Elihu. The water splashed onto Seikh's face as the monsters stomped through it. Soon the sound of the monsters' feet trampling through the water ceased. The silence of the night filled the air. Only the rustling of the monsters' feet through dead leaves could be heard.

As he was being carried face upward, Seikh could see the trees of the woods. They were dark and their branches looked like skinny, crooked fingers ready to grasp him. The moon shone through the trees' black fingers. They were in the Woods of Ebony.

Time slowly passed and Seikh found his thoughts still to be unclear. The green fog must have messed with his mind, leaving him somewhat disoriented and slightly confused. He had no idea how long he had been asleep in the tunnel before the shadow had begun chasing him. How long had he been in the cave? Was it the next night or had it been several days since he had first entered the City of Petra? He knew one thing: if Sangoma and the monsters succeeded in taking him to Surek, his life would be in danger. He also knew that he had to get back to the tunnel and make his way to the Woods of Ivory to find Lamlorde.

Seikh felt he had failed Elihu. He had told him to take a right in the tunnel but instead he had fearfully run away from the shadow and into the small room where the monsters had been. He didn't recall ever seeing a right-hand turn in the tunnel. He now found himself as a captive of a creature known as Sangoma and some wild-looking beasts. He had to go back and find his way to the Woods of Ivory. But how?

As they made their way through the woods, the monsters and Sangoma remained quiet. All that could still be heard were the monsters' footsteps trampling leaves and twigs. Periodically they would stop and the monsters would sniff the air, presumably for gundigans to eat, and then Sangoma would reply, "Come on! There are no gundigans here!"

Hours went by. Finally, the monsters stopped once again to sniff the air. In the distance there was a strange howl. "Gundigans!" the monsters said wryly and with silly giggling. "Let us hunt, Sangoma. Let us hunt!" one said.

"Okay, okay," replied Sangoma. "Some of you come with me to the east to hunt and the rest of you go with Rallee to the west. We'll meet back in thirty minutes." The monsters all agreed.

Seikh heard the rustling of leaves again. After about fifteen minutes, the monsters stopped, sniffed, and looked around. "Hey, I've got an idea!" one of the monsters said. "Let's unwrap the boy and hang him from a tree. The gundigans like Scientian meat. They'll smell him out and then boom! we got ourselves a gundigan!"

"Good idea!" one shouted, and the others agreed.

They unraveled Seikh, tearing off the blanket and scraping the straw and dead leaves onto the ground. Then they took some of the rope from around Seikh's feet and strung him up on a tall tree branch upside down. Dangling in mid-air above the dark, hard ground, blood rushed into Seikh's head. He couldn't help but recollect the events of the past few days. He felt miserable. He was wet, hungry, tired, and now was serving as bait for monsters he had never seen before. His motivation for escaping and then searching for Lamlorde and the cure waned as the pounding of his heart throbbed inside his head. He just wanted everything to be as it was before the night of his vision and seeing the Dreamers burned at the stake. He longed for the old drafty log home where Mother tucked him in at night and Father managed the evening fire. It was safe there. But now everything was different, out of place, dangerous. He was a prisoner. He was alone. No one was near to help him. Seikh yearned for his home, the one that was no more.

8

Pseudomai

T he ornery monsters took cover behind some low-lying bushes several yards away, waiting for some gundigans to find their dinner. Within minutes the groaning and howling of gundigans could be heard nearby. As the moments passed, the howling got louder and closer. Seikh's heart began pounding harder in his chest. He was sweating profusely.

He whispered, "Someone, please. Please help me!"

There was no reply and no sign of help.

If only Mother were here. She would save me. She always protected me.

Not too many yards away, Seikh saw numerous glowing eyes emerge in the darkness. Although he had heard of gundigans, he had never seen one, let alone a pack of them. Mother and Father had always made sure he was not out in the middle of the night in order to keep him safe from the dreadful creatures. Now, in the moonlight, he could make out that they looked like wolves, covered with gray and black hair. They were larger than ordinary wolves, more like the size of cows. As they creeped closer, he could see their fangs as they snarled, growled, and whimpered.

To Seikh's shock and bewilderment, one of the gundigans spoke! "Hoc unum est!" it said. It was a language he did not recognize.

The pack of gundigans surrounded Seikh, nipping at the tip of his head. Seikh began to sway back and forth as hard as he could to elude their fangs. Through the small hole of the sack that covered his face, Seikh saw a branch just several feet higher. If he could just swing high and hard enough, he would be able to escape the gundigans' reach. Taking a deep breath, he swung as hard as he could. As his body was just about to touch the branch, he heard a loud whirling, cracking sound like something rending a thick garment.

Seikh fell to the ground and was now lying in the midst of the gundigan pack! Something had cut through the rope that hung him from the branch. Fearfully, Seikh began rolling as fast as he could to get away from the gundigans. To his surprise, the rope that had tied him had come loose and he found himself free. He stood up, taking off the sack from his head. He saw a bright, shining figure dressed in white just yards away. It stood about seven feet tall. The light emanating from it was white with a faint yellow hue. It was almost too bright to gaze at. Its face was hidden by a white hood, and it was shooting blue glowing arrows at the gundigans. Each arrow penetrated a different gundigan, making the sound of rushing wind and killing each one just like the arrow Surek had used to shoot and kill Elihu. Much further behind the shining figure, Seikh saw the monsters running west further into the woods, shrieking in terror.

Within minutes, every gundigan in the pack had been killed. Seikh stood there, staring at the radiant figure. The mere sight was captivating, even exhilarating. It reminded him of the dream he had in the tunnel when he saw the bright light of The Speech. It also looked similar to Elihu. The figure put down its hands and the glowing blue bow and arrows disappeared. It walked slowly toward Seikh. It spoke with a soft feminine-yet-masculine voice. "There is no more reason to worry. You are safe."

"Are you a Dreamer—a Seer?"

"You can say that," it replied.

"Who are you? And how does this dazzling light shine out from you?"

"They call me Pseudomai. The light proceeds from my nature. What may I call you?"

"I am Seikh. Thank you for saving me."

Pseudomai was now just feet in front of Seikh. The figure's face was still hidden. The white hood from his cloak drooped over his eyes and just to the top of his upper lip. A beard as white as snow was now visible, and his hands were covered with white hair just like Elihu's had been.

"Where did you come from and how did you know I was here? Did you hear my call for help?" Seikh asked as he began to bite his lip.

"I was sent by Lamlorde to rescue you from the pack of gundigans and those monsters, the Pravitas."

"You've seen Lamlorde?" Seikh asked anxiously.

"Why, yes. I was instructed to come here to help you and to give you further directions concerning the cure. Elihu has passed and Lamlorde believed it best to send me in his place." Pseudomai paused, turned, and spoke, "Follow me. I will lead you to where you need to go next."

Seikh normally was hesitant to trust someone he had never met before. But Pseudomai's brilliant light was enchanting and could barely be resisted. He promptly hurried to his side. "First," Pseudomai began to explain, "we must travel further west."

"West? But I thought I must go south to the Woods of Ivory to find Lamlorde. That's what Elihu instructed me. I must go to Lamlorde for he is the only one who has the cure."

"Hmm. The plan has changed, my dear Seikh. Lamlorde no longer holds the cure. He has hidden it in a place where you may now find it—on your own. It is close by. But it can be uncovered only with the heart."

Pseudomai stopped and sat on a large rock, then motioned for Seikh to join him. Seikh moved hesitantly toward the rock, which was now clearly visible because of Pseudomai's radiance. His shining white light was intimidating and made Seikh feel unworthy to approach him.

"Sit next to me," he said solemnly. "We have much to discuss."

The words reminded Seikh of Elihu's first words to him at the cave. It warmed Seikh to hear something familiar, although Pseudomai's voice and aura were somewhat different. In a way, there was also something very familiar about Pseudomai, almost as if he had known him for years. It was a feeling like one gets when thinking of home.

Seikh sat down, though his mind was occupied. "What about Sangoma and the other monsters? Won't they be looking for us? Shouldn't we keep moving?"

"No," he replied tersely. "I have taken care of them for now. Besides, Sangoma is a coward and lacks strength. He has no sense about him. He has run away by now. And the Pravitas are fools and quite inane beasts. They will follow Sangoma wherever he goes—probably back to Surek's castle."

"That's something I don't quite understand," Seikh began thoughtfully. "I have never seen a creature like Sangoma or the Pravitas. I have seen only Scientians, Transmutants, and Dreamers, er, Seers, and only the Transmutants have evolved into something different, but never anything like Sangoma or the Pravitas. Where did they come from? Have they come from a faraway land?"

"You could say that, son," replied Pseudomai. "They have been hidden for some time. They are in the service of Surek. Sangoma is from the race of the Ancients. He has lived for at least four hundred years and serves as Surek's necromancer. He has never evolved. He is still from the Ancient Order."

"What!" Seikh exclaimed as he began making the connection to what Sangoma had told him in the stone room about living for hundreds of years. "How is it possible for someone still to be around from the Ancient Order? I thought they all died hundreds of years ago!"

"They were, except for Sangoma. Enchanting is a practice that leads to all kinds of things that go against nature, especially when someone like him always runs away from any kind of danger. He always uses his powers to escape somehow—even from the plague."

"And what about the Pravitas? They are so ghastly."

"Ah, yes. Those silly brutes are merely Transmutants who have become what they believe they were born as."

"They believe that they were born as one-eyed hideous monsters?"

"Yes." Pseudomai paused and turned toward Seikh for the first time since they sat down. "But what you call 'hideous' another finds comfort and freedom in. Seikh, you will find that what you become is what you already are, so you might as well not fight against nature. In other cases, you can become whatever it is you decide to become. There is change and sometimes there is no change."

"I don't understand," Seikh replied, anxious and annoyed. "What are you saying? Don't speak in riddles. Speak rationally to me."

"Son," he replied with seriousness, "evolving is a natural process and we must let it take its course. We cannot fight change. We must let go and embrace it. All of us must look within ourselves to find our true purpose and meaning and do that which ultimately makes us happy, whether it's being what we were born as or whether we decide to become what we desire. Don't you want to be happy?"

Seikh sat in silence, unsure what to say next. What Pseudomai said was very appealing: he could be whatever he wanted to be and be happy. As he considered Pseudomai's words, Seikh wanted to be finished with the struggle and confusion. He didn't completely understand what was going on anyway. Who really was Elihu? Who was this Lamlorde he was supposed to find? Why had the plans changed? How did he get involved with the search for the cure anyway?

I'm not anyone special.

"If you want to be happy, Seikh, then you need to listen to your own heart. What does your heart tell you?" Pseudomai inquired.

Just then, Seikh was struck with a thought that was as clear as any mathematical concept. "I need to find the cure. Elihu has given me this task and I must fulfill it. Kosmon must be saved. A cure must be found! This is what I must live for now."

Pseudomai placed his hand on Seikh's thigh, "But what does your *heart* tell you, son? Think about it a moment. Be calm and listen. Follow your feelings, not your thoughts."

The words from Pseudomai's lips were like morsels. Seikh sat calmly and breathed deeply. He felt relaxed. He slowly took another breath. It felt like he was inhaling something lighter than air. It was soothing. His mind began to feel numb. As he exhaled, his heart ached, yearning to be released from this burden Elihu placed upon him. Seikh's eyes teared up and he began to sob. He looked at Pseudomai, whose shining light was now surrounding him and penetrating him. "I just, I just want to go home."

"There, there, my son," Pseudomai said sympathetically, placing his arm around him. Seikh laid his head on Pseudomai's shoulder. "Seikh, Lamlorde knew what your heart most desired, so he sent me with this message. Don't you see? The cure is in your heart—it's whatever you want to do most. And that's the cure for Kosmon. When we all go where our heart leads us, we become who we are supposed to be. Then the violence and the fighting will dissipate, and the plague will be no more. When we love one another and accept each other for who we are—whatever it is—we become free. The cure is not some kind of potion to be taken; it is recognizing that we need to follow our own passions and desires in our heart and accept one another. Tolerance. Acceptance."

Seikh's tears began to dry, and he sat up. "Do you really think I can go home? Is that what Lamlorde would really want?"

"Lamlorde has given us all permission. Do you want to go home?"

"I think so," replied Seikh. Pseudomai placed his hand on his head and a yellow hue softly glowed around his face. "Yes. Yes, my heart says I want to go home."

"Then come with me. I know where it is. We will have to go to the West—through the Woods and over the hills. It's just a day's journey. But soon enough you will find yourself at home in the comfort of familiar surroundings."

"But Mother and Father will not be there. What about them? It just won't be the same without them," Seikh replied sadly.

"No. Your father will not be there." Pseudomai paused thoughtfully and then continued, "But perhaps your mother will be."

Seikh sat up in shock. "How can that be? She's dead," he spoke solemnly.

"No, son. You *think* she is dead. I have information that she is still alive."

"Mother is alive?"

"Yes."

Seikh couldn't believe it. Perhaps everything could be like it had been before! Father would not be there, but at least Mother would be, and they would be happy in their log home. "Do you know where my mother is?"

"Yes, I have been told where she is. She is being held in the dungeons of Kosmon, beneath Surek's castle."

Seikh's hope of seeing Mother plummeted as fast as it had risen. The very person who was after him held his mother in custody. How would he ever see her again? "Is there a way to rescue her?"

"Well, now that will be very difficult. The dungeons of Kosmon hold the most insane people—those who believe their hallucinations are real and are a danger to society—and so they must be heavily guarded. The doors of the dungeons are protected by some of the most ferocious creatures, not to mention their weapons make them nearly impossible to get past."

"But we must try!" said Seikh emphatically. "Home will not be the same without her. Besides, she is my mother, and I must save her!"

Pseudomai was now standing, looking off into the distance. He appeared to be thinking deeply about Seikh's proposal. He turned slowly toward Seikh and spoke softly, yet intentionally. "If that's your heart's desire, then we must go to her so the two of you can be reunited and be at home with each other once again. We will have to travel even farther than the eastern foothills. Surek's castle lies just on the other side of Black Mountain. The journey will be difficult. There are many difficult terrains to scale between here and there. Besides this, once we reach the castle, it will be nearly impossible to penetrate as it lies embedded in the rock of Black Mountain."

"Yes, I know. But it will be worth it. My true desire will be fulfilled, and I will avoid the plague and help Kosmon do the same. It's just like you said—true happiness is the cure for the plague. If we can all do our own part by finding our own purpose, then death may never happen again. By saving my mother, I can save myself."

"And so it is," Pseudomai chortled. Pseudomai began walking and then glanced over his shoulder at Seikh. "We must be on our way. The journey will be long and difficult, and we have to get supplies, especially food and canteens for water." Pseudomai paused. "Seikh, your old log home is on the way. That will be the best place to get food. Whatever is there we must take."

Seikh nodded. He didn't want to go back, not now, without Mother or Father, but he knew they must. It was the only place to prepare for their long journey ahead.

9

Philo

T he night was cold, with a mist hanging in the air. Lying on his back, Seikh stared at the moon as it shone dimly through passing clouds. Pseudomai stood against a large tree, sleeping. Seikh thought it was strange that he could sleep so well standing up, but Pseudomai explained that's how all Seers slept. Seikh's spot on the ground was most uncomfortable, but he had agreed to stop for several hours to rest before moving on to his old house to get supplies. Sleep, however, was one thing that Seikh was not going to get. Every time his eyes closed all he could think about was his mother being held at Surek's castle and how to rescue her.

As he lay there staring into the night sky, he thought about what Pseudomai had said concerning his mother—he had only *thought* she was dead.

I would have sworn I saw her killed. What if the same is true of Father? Could he be alive as well?

No, it couldn't be. That would be too good to be true. Besides, Pseudomai would have told him if Father were also alive.

Seikh rolled over onto his side.

"Can't sleep?" Pseudomai questioned, his voice piercing the darkness.

Seikh turned back to answer Pseudomai. As he looked at him, he noticed the light that beamed from him was not as radiant. It seemed to have dimmed. "What happened to your light?"

"The light that shines forth from me doesn't always shine with the same intensity. There are times that I can control it, such as now, for the sake of hiding. My radiance will make it too easy for Surek and his men to find us, so I must dim it. During the day you will not even notice my

radiance for it will be lost in the light of the day." Seikh sat up and Pseudomai approached him. "Perhaps we should get going. It will be light in a few
hours. If we can get to your house to pick up our supplies before the first
light, the better."

"Yeah, I agree." Seikh rose from the ground, dusting himself off and
stretching. "If this is going to be a long trip, perhaps we should attempt to
find some transportation? Do you know where we can find some horses?"

"Horses will be difficult to come by. We will have to steal them if we
want to go undetected. By now, Surek has surely spread the word that we
are wanted criminals, and everyone will be on the lookout for us."

"Well, you're a Seer. Don't you have powers to help us locate some
horses and do it quietly?" Seikh asked somewhat indignantly.

Pseudomai chuckled. "Well, it doesn't quite work like that. I have no
more powers than you have. Seers simply have dreams; they have no supernatural powers."

"You certainly have powers, don't you? How do you explain the blue
bow and arrows? They just appeared when you needed them and then disappeared when you didn't."

"Hmm. Yes." Pseudomai picked up a stick from the ground and looked
it over. "Weapons like that are not due to any supernatural powers that I
have. They are given to me by the Greater Power when I need them."

"The Greater Power?" inquired Seikh.

"The Greater Power is what gives us Seers the dreams we have. He
guides us and gives us weapons when we need them."

Seikh looked inquisitively at him. "Is the Greater Power the same as
The Speech?"

Pseudomai's stance straightened. "How do you know about The
Speech?" Seikh detected that he was somewhat disturbed by the question.

"Elihu told me about him."

Seikh hesitated before saying anything more. He thought about the
prophecy Elihu had told him about and how he was to listen to The Speech.
He felt a pit in his stomach. He had turned against all this by deciding to
save his mother. But was the prophecy true? Seikh didn't want it to be.

I am no one special. And I am certainly not some kind of "chosen one."

Seikh felt it better not to mention this prophecy, or even the dream he
had of The Speech, to Pseudomai. He buried these thoughts deep into his
subconscious, hoping they would go away.

"Ah, Elihu!" Pseudomai blurted out. "He spoke to you before he died, did he? You must be careful whom you listen to, Seikh. Although he was a Seer, his old age got the better of him. He became somewhat delusional and confused. Whatever he told you of The Speech, do not take it to heart. The Greater Power is certainly not the same as The Speech. The Speech is a power who is attempting to take control of Kosmon. He's a deceiver. You must listen to the Greater Power, for he is indeed much greater! Elihu must have confused the two in his old age." He paused. "We must now focus on getting your mother back." He turned and tossed the stick he had been holding to Seikh. "Take this! It may be the only thing that makes our journey more endurable."

"A stick?"

"Not just any stick. A *walking* stick." Pseudomai snickered, bent over, and picked up another stick for himself. "There! Now we are both ready for this long journey." He rubbed the long stick in his hands and thrust the butt of it to the ground. "Nevertheless, if we come across some horses, we shall make use of them."

Seikh and Pseudomai walked through the Woods of Ebony for a few hours. They traveled through the thickest parts without being detected, and in fact did not even spot another person or creature. As the light of day began to seep faintly through the treetops, thick clouds lay as a blanket in the sky and the mist remained in the air, making it a gray and gloomy early morning—a typical day in Kosmon. Dew covered the black bark of the trees, making it look like tar was oozing down them. The air was still cool, and it motivated Seikh to reach his old log home more quickly to retrieve additional clothes and a jacket. He was also hungry. It felt as if he hadn't eaten in days. As Seikh thought about it, it may have been days or even weeks since he had his last meal. He had no idea how long he had been in the cave and the time that had transpired since his meeting with Elihu. His lack of food and sleep had made him weak. He began to wonder if his thoughts and decisions were being affected. Even his eyesight seemed to be playing tricks on him. He thought several times that he had seen a dark figure lurking around trees and following behind them as they journeyed.

Pseudomai led the way through the woods, up and over numerous hills, and across a lot of flat land as well. The trees were as thick as ever. As they approached a steep, small hill, Seikh recognized this part of the woods.

He had played there when he was younger. There were small pine trees that lined the top of the hill and fruit trees around both sides. There was a clearing between the pines and fruit trees where he would often lay, eating fruit and staring at the gloomy sky, always wondering about the meaning of life.

They began scaling the small hill to the short pines. As they reached the top, Pseudomai held his hand up, indicating for Seikh to halt. Between the short pines, just one hundred yards away, Seikh saw the edge of the other side of the clearing. Nestled just inside the woods he could barely make out his old log home. It appeared silent and lonely. The windows were dark. It looked as if it were frowning and had no life in it.

As Seikh stood there with his gaze fixed on his heart's most ardent desire—home—his thoughts raced back to his childhood. He remembered how his mother would play with him on the old wooden floor of the homely cabin. The creaks of the floorboards would often serve as musical notes. Father would bounce up and down on them, creating humorous lyrics.

"How do you catch a toad, catch a toad, catch a toad?" went his favorite song in between the creaks. "Not running over it in the road, in the road, in the road."

Seikh could almost hear his father's voice singing and his laughter between verses.

His thoughts traveled back to how his mother would physically change from season to season. Father never did, but Mother would. He never saw her evolve into a different creature. She would always transform at night or somewhere in secret, away from Seikh. He remembered how she once looked a lot like Father, a Scientian.

"They are a good-looking couple," people would say about his mother and father.

But then mother began evolving, slowly over time, into a mix between a horse and a Scientian. She always said this was because she began to learn a lot about herself. She explained that her outer looks changed to reflect who she really was on the inside. Father always celebrated with mother for the changes she went through.

"Mother is becoming an individual. She's being true to herself, learning how to identify," he would say.

Now the house he stared at through the pine trees was neither home to Mother or Father. There were no songs in the house. Father was dead. There was no Mother waiting to play with him. She was a captive in Surek's castle.

"Seikh!" Pseudomai declared softly. "Where is your mind, boy? We must get to the house. But we must be careful. It looks like someone has been there. The windows appear to have been busted out, and there's a little smoke coming from the chimney. To be careful, we will walk along the tree line until we reach it. Follow me."

Seikh followed Pseudomai to the east, hugging the tree line. The day had broken, and more light made it easier to navigate through the trees. The mist had begun to dissipate which made the house more visible. When they got to within about twenty yards of the house, Pseudomai motioned for Seikh to get down. They crawled to a spot beneath the living room window. Sure enough, the window had been busted out. Shattered glass was scattered on the ground. With their backs against the house, they sat listening for any sounds. Seikh didn't hear any voices or commotion inside, but a hint of smoke was coming from the fireplace.

Pseudomai peeked slowly and carefully into the house through the broken window. He then dropped back to the ground. "I don't see anyone. Let's make our way through the back door."

Stepping up to the rickety wooden entryway, just to the left of the window, Pseudomai tried the knob and it fell into his hand. As little broken pieces of metal and screws fell to the floor of the house, the door creaked open. A mouse scurried across the room. At the same time, Seikh thought he saw a shadowy figure duck behind the door that led into his bedroom.

"What was that?" Seikh whispered with anticipation, his heart beginning to palpitate.

"What?"

"Didn't you see that shadow that darted into my bedroom?"

"No, I saw nothing but the mouse."

Seikh slowly stepped toward the bedroom. Just as he was about to nudge the door open, a floorboard squeaked. Without warning the door thrust open, knocking Seikh to the floor. The figure dashed past Pseudomai and was headed toward the back door when Pseudomai extended his hand. Something like a rope, glowing blue, appeared and wrapped itself around the figure's ankles like a lasso. Pseudomai yanked on the rope and brought the figure down with a thud.

"Please!" cried out the figure, face down. "Don't hurt me!"

Seikh recognized the voice. It sounded like his good friend Philo. Seikh sprung to his feet and hurried to the figure's side.

"Philo?" he called out, turning him over. "Is that you?"

"Seikh?" Philo, lying on his back, looked intently into his eyes.

"Yes. It's me. What are you doing here? Are you okay?"

"Yeah. I'm fine," he said breathlessly. Rising clumsily from the dusty cabin floor and rubbing his ankles, he huffed in exasperation. "I've been living here since my parents were taken by Surek and his men."

"Your parents taken? Why? What's going on?"

"I don't know. All I know is that Surek's men came to my house one night about two weeks ago and took my parents away. When I heard them breaking into the house I got scared and ran away. I escaped through the window in my bedroom. I came here first to find you, but I found that Surek's men had been here. The windows were broken, and the doors had been busted open. The entire house had been ransacked. And you and your parents were gone!"

Philo lunged toward Seikh and held onto him, sobbing. "Oh, Seikh! I am so glad to see you, my good friend. I am so glad you are alright!"

Seikh held onto him, feeling his friend's tense body relax in his arms.

Philo backed away from Seikh, taking him by the arms. "We must get out of here and find a safer place to stay for a while. Surek will eventually find me, and you too!"

"Yes, I know. We already have a plan," Seikh said looking toward Pseudomai. "It will keep us on the move. But we must rescue my mother first. Surek captured her. We are going to look for her at his castle."

"We?" asked Philo looking around seeing no one. "*We* who?"

"Pseudomai and me," Seikh replied. "Meet Pseudomai the Seer. He saved me from a pack of gundigans." Seikh nodded in Pseudomai's direction, but Philo appeared confused and disoriented, as if unaware of Pseudomai's presence.

"Oh!" Philo said after rubbing his eyes as if to see more clearly. "Nice to meet you!" He held out his hand confidently to shake Pseudomai's hand. Pseudomai returned the gesture and nodded his hooded head. Philo turned to Seikh again and spoke in a commanding voice, "You cannot go to Surek's castle! It is way too dangerous! They will find you and kill you!"

Looking at Philo, Seikh spoke grimly, "But he has my mother. I must save her."

"But how?" Philo inquired.

"That's a long story." Seikh paused, stood up, and reached out his hand toward Philo. "Come with us. Help save my mother. We could use your help, and we can help find your parents, too."

Philo grabbed Seikh's hand. "Of course, friend. Anything for you, and my parents."

Seikh faced Pseudomai. "What do you say? Can we have another tag-along?"

"I don't see why not. Three strands of a rope are stronger than two."

"It's settled then. All we need is a plan to get into Surek's castle."

"I can certainly help," Philo chirped with a slight grin. "I have been to Surek's castle before. I know my way around."

His sense of self-worth was visible in his posture. Seikh was glad to have his confident friend with them.

After a few hours of packing clothes, food, and other supplies, Seikh, Pseudomai, and Philo were ready to make their plan. Philo explained that he had been inside Surek's castle just the year before. His class from school had taken a tour of it. Every year, a different class would visit the castle to learn about the history and greatness of Kosmon. The class chosen for the trip was always excited because it took a week to travel to the castle and back. It was an entire week off from school. Unfortunately, Seikh's class had never been chosen.

Philo recounted to Seikh and Pseudomai the castle's museum, which contained many ancient Kosmonian artifacts—swords and suits of armor used in war, original manuscripts of the Annals of Kosmon, and items from the extinct Ancient Order. The items from the Ancient Order were displayed as "a reminder of how things used to be and never ought to be again" as the plaque that hung on the wall indicated.

Philo recalled much of the layout of the castle and museum, and with a large sheet of paper and a pencil, sitting on the old creaky wooden floor of the log house, he was able to sketch most of the first floor of the castle.

"But mother is most likely not on the first floor," replied Seikh after gazing at the layout. "She and your parents, if they are there, are probably in the lower dungeons where they keep the delusional people."

"Lower dungeons where they keep the delusional people? I don't remember any lower floor. And who are these people you are talking about? Surely if they existed, I would know about them," Philo asserted.

Seikh looked at Pseudomai. "Tell him, Pseudomai."

"Not many know about the lower dungeons," replied Pseudomai. "As I told Seikh before, they are for the most insane people. They hallucinate and see visions, and they think they are real. They continuously blabber about seeing things 'as they really are.' Surek had the dungeons built to keep these people from corrupting and endangering Kosmonians. The dungeons are actually underground beneath the castle and are heavily guarded."

"Wait a minute!" Philo interrupted. "Now I remember! I knew my memory was not that bad. There is a spiral staircase on the north end of the castle. A large, locked gate blocks the staircase. I thought it just led to an old garden or something and didn't pay much attention to it. That's the way to the dungeons!"

"How do you remember all this?" asked Seikh.

"If I see it, I remember it," said Philo proudly. "My memory is one of the best."

"That may be the initial way to the dungeons," interjected Pseudomai, "but it's highly unlikely that only a large, locked gate stands in the way. It's been said that Pravitas, gundigans, and other monsters guard the dungeons with heavy armor—and their formidable strength. And this is not to mention that Surek's high guards are probably protecting the castle. The staircase must be just the beginning of the pathway to the dungeons."

"You're right," responded Philo thoughtfully. "There must be some way we can sneak into the castle unnoticed."

Pseudomai pointed to the top of Philo's sketch. "We could enter through the back of the castle by going around Black Mountain on the north. Surely there are entrances in the rear."

"Yes, we will have to scope it out once we get there. I'm glad I thought of it!" Philo replied, pounding Seikh on the back.

"Right! Well, it sounds like we have a beginning to a plan. We'd better go." Seikh spoke anxiously, grasping the bag he had filled with supplies. "I don't want to waste any more time. The longer Mother is there, the more likely she is in danger. All I want to do is get her back. That's my mission now."

Pseudomai smiled and nodded at Seikh. They picked up their bags and scurried through the back door of the log house and out into the gloomy Woods of Ebony.

10

Zoe

T he further east they traveled, the thicker and blacker the woods became. Trees stood about four feet apart—sometimes less—in every
direction. The trees crowded out most of the daylight. Their tops made a
dark, towering canopy. If it were not for knowing about what time of day it
was, they could have mistaken it for dusk.

"What's with these woods? The trees are so dense and eerily dark,
darker than usual," commented Seikh.

"These woods have been like this for as long as I can remember," Philo
replied matter-of-factly. "But you're right. They do seem darker than usual.
I did kind of notice that. Ever since the massacre at Hinnom, the Woods
and the sky seem darker—*everything* seems so ominous."

"The massacre at Hinnom?" Seikh inquired. "The Hinnom Meadow?"

"Yes. Didn't you hear about it? Everyone knows what happened there!"
Philo was following closely alongside Pseudomai and Seikh, occasionally
bumping up against the blackened trees of the forest. The sound of dead
leaves gently crunched beneath their feet with each step.

"If you are talking about the Dreamers who were burned at the stakes
by the Scientians, I was there!" exclaimed Seikh.

"You were there?" Shocked, Philo stopped in his tracks, pulling Seikh
to look at him. "How did you escape?"

Seikh recognized the implication in his friend's voice. What Philo really meant was how did he escape since he looked mostly like a Dreamer.
Ever since they had been very young, Philo had always commented how
much he thought Seikh looked like a Dreamer.

Seikh wriggled quickly out of Philo' grasp. "Just because I might *look* like a Dreamer doesn't mean I am one!"

"No, I mean—"

"I know what you meant. How did I escape being killed since I am a Dreamer myself? Like I said, just because I may look like one doesn't mean I am one!"

"Come, you two!" Pseudomai called out. He was now about fifty yards in front of them and halfway up an incline where the trees grew thinner. "It's no time to be quibbling."

Both turned and looked at him. He was already making his way up the small hill again.

"What do you think of him?" asked Philo, quieting his voice to a whisper. He had an aura of self-righteousness about him.

"Pseudomai?"

"Yeah. I mean, do you know him? Do you trust him?" Philo questioned.

"He saved me from a pack of gundigans. And he has helped me see more clearly about some things. And, besides, he is going to help me save my mother."

"But do you *trust* him?" Philo's tone was condescending. "How well do you really know him?"

"Why? You are acting awfully suspicious. That's not like you." Seikh glanced at his friend, who had a look of concern on his face.

"He gleams, doesn't he? I mean with light, right?"

"Well, yes. But you can't see it very well in the daylight. He gets brighter as dark falls. Why? Why are you suspicious? You are acting like he's a part of a conspiracy."

"He has a shimmer of yellow to him, too, doesn't he?" Philo asked as if he already knew the answer.

Seikh was now irritated and quite disgusted. "Yes, he does! Mostly he glows with bright white with a slight yellow shimmer around the edges. Why? Quit playing with me and tell me what is making you so suspicious!"

A cry from the top of hill interrupted their conversation. "Get down! Take cover behind the brush!"

Cresting over the hill were six large black animals that resembled oxen with horns protruding from their heads. They were running fast toward Pseudomai. On top of each animal rode a creature wearing black.

"Surek's men!" Philo called out. He grabbed Seikh by the arm and began running down the hill and leaped behind some brush. Peeking around a thorny bush, Seikh saw Pseudomai using his glowing blue rope to trip up the oxen.

"Stay here," Philo commanded, gasping for air. "And if you need to, run and hide! I will find you. Just run!"

"Wait! Where are you going?"

"To fight them!"

Philo jumped out from behind the brush and ran up the hill. As he was running, he reached his hand into the bag he had strapped onto his back. He pulled out a long thin sword. It glowed yellow with red around the edges. He began lunging and swinging it at the oxen, swiping and then cutting them down with loud zipping sounds. Surek's men floated gently and swiftly off the fallen oxen and engaged Philo with their red glowing swords that appeared out of thin air. Philo moved with vigilance and confidence, side-stepping every jab and thrust that came from Surek's men. He dropped one of Surek's men and then another and was now fighting just two.

Pseudomai was battling the other two men, using his rope as a whip. Dropping them both to their knees, he drew his blue glowing bow and arrow and shot each in turn. Upon impact, the men appeared to melt and then disappear.

Just as Pseudomai had shot the two men, Philo plunged his sword deep into the final two men. Philo lowered his arms in exhaustion, and the glowing yellow and red blade disappeared. He was left holding the sword's golden handle. He looked toward the brush where Seikh had been hiding, placed the sword's handle back into his pack, and began walking toward him.

"It's all clear!" Philo called out, approaching Seikh.

"How did you do that?" Seikh questioned in astonishment.

"It's a long story," he replied nonchalantly. "Perhaps I will tell you about it sometime."

"Yes, indeed," retorted Pseudomai who was now approaching them from behind. "That was some very nice swordsmanship. Only Surek's men know how to wield a sword like that."

"Like I said, it's a long story." Philo began slowly walking back up the hill.

"Just like how you happened to retrieve such a mighty weapon as a golden phanos sword?" Pseudomai questioned seriously.

Philo paused. "Yes, for sure. Perhaps the story is for another day. We'd better get moving before more of Surek's men arrive. And they certainly will arrive." Again, he began walking up the hill, but then he stopped. "Perhaps we should go *around* the hill this time?"

"Yeah, good idea," replied Seikh. "We should take cover in the woods that go around the hill so we can see if anyone is coming this time."

"Lead on, Pseudomai," Philo commanded, still out of breath. "Seikh and I will follow."

The hill was much larger than Seikh had thought. It had been at least four hours and they were still making their way around it. It was now dusk, and the cool, misty air had returned. Pseudomai led Philo and Seikh through the dark woods around the edge of the steep hill, whacking down branches with his walking stick to make a path through the thick brush. They had not run into any more of Surek's men along the way, but Seikh felt as if they were being watched. He couldn't stop biting the inside of his cheek. Pseudomai tried to ease Seikh's nerves several times but to no avail. Seikh couldn't help but think that somehow Surek was keeping his eye on them.

They continued through the woods unabated. Dusk began to fall. The trees had become like dark, tall shadows standing around them. Seikh looked to his left toward the hill. It was beginning to slope downward. Brown and black grass covered it. It was matted down and looked like it had been trampled by an army. Several trees sprinkled the bottom of the hill, giving an appearance of soldiers slouching over with their arms dangling to the ground, marching up the incline. The black bark and and the appearance of oozing tar gave them an eerie and disturbing appearance.

Seikh sighed, relieved to be finally coming to the other side of the hill. "Finally! I thought we would never get to the end of this hill. That was the largest one I have ever seen!"

"That's no hill," Philo replied. "It's a plateau. And an exceptionally large one at that!" He squinted, looking toward it. He seemed to be in deep thought and then he pulled out something to eat from his pack. "If I had to guess," he said, munching, as the scent of dried meat permeated the air, "this must be the Polemos Plateau. If so, then we still have at least another day's travel if not two."

"Yes, you are correct, Philo," Pseudomai commented. His radiance began to illuminate their surroundings. "You know your geography quite well. Unfortunately, it's getting dark, and it would be unwise to continue. We ought to set up camp. It looks as if the forest is going to get thicker."

Feeling exhausted from the day's travel and excitement, Seikh consented. Philo didn't appear disagreeable, so they found a small clearing at the bottom of the plateau and began to set up camp. Seikh and Philo got to work looking for wood to build a fire, while Pseudomai provided light for their search. Pseudomai's outlying yellow glow seemed more intense than it had the night before. His glow, however, was not as white and magnificent overall. It appeared dimmer near his body, and the yellow seemed to penetrate further into him.

Seikh and Philo wandered into the woods to find kindling for a fire. As Seikh bent over to pick up some sticks, Philo knelt close and whispered, "Follow me."

Without another sound, he stood up, gently tugging on Seikh's elbow, attempting to lead him further away from Pseudomai who was looking the opposite direction.

Pretending to be searching for firewood, Philo led Seikh about fifty yards further into the woods.

"What are you doing?" Seikh whispered indignantly.

"Haven't you noticed Pseudomai's light? How it's more yellow and less white?"

"Yeah," Seikh replied, looking over his shoulder. "So what?"

"There's something more to him than he's telling us."

Craning his neck, Seikh closed in on him. "Well, maybe he's dimming it so as not to attract attention. Seers do that, you know."

"Who told you that? Pseudomai?" Philo's accusatory tone could not be missed.

Without hesitation, Seikh quipped back, "Philo, you have been so suspicious of him from the beginning. Tell me, what is the deal?"

"I think he may be—"

"Seikh! Philo!"

"Over here, looking for wood!" Philo cried out.

Before they could turn around, Pseudomai was directly behind them. "Perhaps we have enough wood. We should light a fire and get some sleep. It's getting cold and we will need to get up early."

He looked at them intently, almost as if he were peering into their souls, and then he made his way back to the camp site. Philo and Seikh followed behind him.

The night was intensely black and Seikh became more unsettled. Not being able to see immediately in front of him made him nervous. He was glad when Pseudomai lit the kindling and stoked the wood into a blazing fire. The flickering flames danced and lit up the surrounding trees.

Seikh dug into his backpack, grabbing some blankets and laying them on the ground for a bed. Philo made his bed just catty corner to him and Pseudomai postured himself against a tree, standing to sleep as usual.

As Seikh burrowed into his warm blankets, he glanced toward Philo. He was already nestled deep into his bed, asleep. His head barely peeked out from underneath his covers, and he lay motionless upon a pillow made of leaves. His golden hair reflected the light of the fire, which gave a kind of angelic aura to him. It seemed purer and more lucent than Pseudomai's radiance. Philo seemed quite different from when Seikh grew up playing with him. He mulled over his friend's entrance into his day. Although Seikh was overjoyed to find his good friend at his house, Philo was indeed different. He had always been the mischievous and playful of the two of them. He now seemed serious, resolute, and confident.

Seikh awoke to darkness. The fire had gone out. The black of the night was so thick it hid the trees around him. Pseudomai's shimmering light was no longer glowing. Perhaps he dimmed it for safety. Seikh sat up and looked around intently, trying to see anything he could. But every which way he turned his head he saw nothing but blackness. As anxiety began to swell within him, he looked about furiously for any kind of light. He jerked his head to the left and then to the right. His eye caught a glimpse of a faint silvery glow hovering near the ground a few yards away. Focusing his eyes upon the dull source of light, Seikh discerned it was coming from Philo's bag which he had placed at his feet. Seikh sat staring at the luminosity coming from Philo's bag.

"Take up and read," a soft voice said.

Frightened, Seikh looked around. Where was the voice coming from?

"Take up and read," it said again.

Looking suspiciously and with trepidation at the shimmering white light, Seikh found enough courage to ask, "Me?"

In response, the voice repeated slowly with every word articulated with intentionality, "Take. Up. And. Read."

Without further contemplation, Seikh cautiously arose from the ground and crawled sluggishly toward the bag. He could barely make out Philo's silhouette as the white light faintly illuminated the immediate surroundings. Philo was sound asleep with his covers over his head. Seikh looked to the right and then all around. Where was Pseudomai? Was anyone looking?

Seikh looked down at the bag and began to carefully untie the flap which kept the silvery glow partially hidden. Seikh drew the flap open and reached inside, grabbing what felt like a heavy book. As he slipped it out, the light became brighter. The book was large, and it was clear like glass. Seikh could see through its front cover to the back of the book. He wiggled his fingers on the backside to see if he could really see through it or whether his eyes were tricking him. His hands and fingers glided smoothly over its surface, and he could see clearly through the entire book. There were no pages. On the front cover was a single word engraved in white: *Zoe.*

"Open. And. Read," said the mysterious voice again.

Seikh fumbled the book in his hands, looking for a way to open it. He slid his fingers down the right edge and it immediately flipped open. Pages began turning furiously and came to a stop in the middle of the translucent tome. The only words on the page read, "You are in the Infinite. Take courage. The Finite will be overcome. You have been chosen."

11

The Scarlet Riders

"Seikh! What are you doing up?"

Pseudomai's light pierced the darkness from behind him. Seikh quickly turned. Pseudomai was hovering, staring down at him with his usual stoic expression, with his hood covering all but his mouth.

"Oh, nothing," Seikh replied, stumbling over his words and shifting his stance to cover up the bag. "I just got hungry when I woke up and thought maybe Philo had something in his bag."

"Hmm. Well, I suggest you get it quickly. We ought to be going. First light will be soon."

"Yeah. I'll wake Philo."

Pseudomai turned and walked away, leaving Seikh in the dark. He turned and looked at Philo's bag. The book was gone.

Where did it go?

He frantically searched around the area, shuffling around blankets and dead leaves.

"Hey! What are you doing?" Philo groggily sat up from his bed. "That's my bag! Leave it alone!"

"I'm hungry," Seikh snapped. "You got any food?"

"Yeah, but you don't have to rummage through my private things to find some," Philo said, indignant.

"Well, *excuse me*, my good friend!" Seikh replied sarcastically.

Philo looked agitated, his face elongating. "I have some important things in my bag, and they should not be messed with."

"Like that nice-looking, shiny sword?"

"Yeah, right."

Grabbing the bag from Seikh, Philo began stuffing it with his blankets.

"Which you still have yet to explain," Seikh added. "How did you come by retrieving it?" He popped a piece of granola in his mouth which he had snuck from Philo's bag before it was ripped from his hands. "You know, Pseudomai is right: you must have done *something* quite fascinating to obtain a phanos sword. I'm only aware of Surek's high guards having weapons like that. What did you do? Kill one?"

"Ha!" Philo bellowed. "Do you think that taking the life of a high guard is *that* easy? Only well-trained swordsman can do such a thing."

"Well, you seemed to take down those beasts yesterday quite easily."

"Sometimes things look easier than they really are."

"C'mon. Be honest with me. Where did you learn such fighting and how did you get that sword? You've obviously been trained."

"Yes, please tell." Pseudomai's voice trickled eerily into their discussion, frightening both of them.

"Geez, Pseudomai! You gotta stop sneaking up behind us like that! You are going to kill me." Seikh held his chest while his heart pounded.

"Alright. If you guys really want to know," Philo began, exasperation in his tone as he sat down on a nearby rock, "and if we really have the time—"

"You're right. We probably don't have time for it now. But you're going to tell us your adventure sometime." Seikh was anxious to hear it, but he knew they needed to pack up.

Philo finished stuffing his bag with his belongings while Seikh prepared his things. Pseudomai stood and waited.

"Where do we go from here?" Seikh glanced at Pseudomai. His light was now shining brightly. "And how much farther do we have to go before we reach Surek's castle?"

"We must continue heading east. First, we will encounter the tar pits not too far from here. Then we will come upon a few villages on the outskirts of the Black Mountain where Surek's castle stands. It may take just a few days more to get there." Pseudomai reached for his walking stick that was leaning against a tree. "Finish packing and let's go. It's beginning to get light out."

After gathering all their belongings, they headed east through the woods. Traveling no more than about fifty yards, the trees abruptly ended. What looked like a beach covered with tar lay in front of a large clearing in which large black puddles littered the ground. The sky was bleak and grayer than the day before, and it was littered with ominous dark clouds that seemed to be grasping for the ground. An awful stench filled the air. Something like putrid flesh.

Pseudomai stopped.

Seikh exclaimed, "Ugh! What's that terrible smell?"

Philo halted. His shoulders slumped. "The tar pits."

Seikh swiveled his head to the left and right. He noticed the perfect line the trees made behind them. "Look! Isn't that odd? The trees just stop, like someone just hacked them down. And look over there! There are three perfect lines of trees that get shorter as they get closer to the tar pits." Just to the left a line of trees stood about Seikh's height. Another line stood about ten feet high and another about twenty feet.

Seikh walked cautiously to one of the tar pits immediately in front of him. He bent down and looked intently into the black, mirrorlike surface of the tar. He saw his dirty reflection. His hair was messy, and it was whiter than he had remembered. He had dark circles under his eyes. As he stared at his awful complexion, the tar began to bubble as if it were beginning to boil. Slowly a crimson hue appeared, glowing in the tar. The hue became scarlet and formed into a skull. Seikh jumped back.

"Uh, guys. There's something in this tar, and I don't think it's friendly." Seikh turned. "Guys?"

An uncanny silence hovered around them. Philo was holding his finger to his lips to hush Seikh.

"What's wrong?" Seikh's voice was barely audible.

Philo and Pseudomai motioned for Seikh to come to them.

Slowly, Seikh approached them. "What is going on?"

"Shh…" Philo slowly put his finger to his lips again. He craned his neck and whispered into Seikh's ear. "These aren't trees, you fool!"

In shock, Seikh drew back and looked around. In a flash, he saw that Philo was right. The trees were an army of some sort which had marched out of the tar pits. This is why they were in lines and looked like they had arms draping to the ground. The tar that covered the trees had come from the pits.

Pseudomai leaned toward Seikh and Philo, barely whispering. "These trees are an army probably under the control of Surek. Surely they have been watching our every move since last night. We may have a fight on our hands."

Crack!

A flash of lightning streaked from the dark clouds to the ground.

Crack!

Another bolt stretched across the sky. Thunder rolled and billowed around them. The trees began to shake, and the earth quaked. The clouds shifted violently and swirled into shapes that looked like hands. They hovered above the tar pits and then thrust themselves into the thick black resin, splattering black ooze like an explosion. The cloud hands, their fingers clasped, reappeared, drawing trees from the pits. The trees came alive. They carried figures wearing scarlet robes and holding golden glowing rods. Red skulls protruded from the tops of their robes. They began to charge and joust.

Seikh screeched, "Pseudomai! What do we do?"

The trembling trees around them came alive and began charging and swiping their limbs at them.

"Get behind me, Seikh!" yelled Philo as he pulled his phanos sword from his pack.

Seikh lurched behind Philo. The yellow and red light of the phanos sword gleamed intensely and flashed as Philo struck the arms of the trees which grasped for them. Limbs were hacked, splintering into the air.

The Scarlet Riders were now on top of them, and the stench of rotten flesh leaked from their presence. They thrusted their rods at Seikh, and small bolts of lightning sparked from the tips, shocking him on the arms and legs. Seikh screamed in pain.

With a swift stroke of his sword, Philo cut through the golden rods, destroying them with a sound of shattering glass. The Scarlet Riders leaped off the trees. One after the other, Philo cut them through, each disappearing with a flash. But more Scarlet Riders and trees kept coming.

A tree limb clutched Seikh and threw him to the ground. Seikh's head began throbbing horribly. He felt around for anything he could use as a weapon. His hand fell upon one of the hacked tree limbs and he began swinging it, hitting the tree and knocking off smaller limbs. But it was not good enough to stop it or even slow it down from its attack. The tree wrapped numerous limbs around him. He wrestled and struggled to break free from its torturous grip. A zipping noise pierced the air. Philo's sword cut through the limbs, setting Seikh free.

"Follow me!" Philo took off running.

Seikh ran as fast as he could, following Philo closely. They darted around the tar pits while Philo hacked numerous trees grasping for them. They slowly began to outrun the trees. The Scarlet Riders seemed unable to maneuver effectively around the tar pits. One by one, the trees fell into the ponds of black tar and began disappearing.

"Look!" cried Seikh, stopping in bewilderment. "The trees are falling into the pits!"

"Don't stop now!" Philo turned and grabbed Seikh by the arm. His arm stung. It had a gash and was bleeding. "We are almost there!"

"Where?"

"You'll see!" Philo took off, dragging Seikh alongside him.

They raced around the tar pits, jumping over scattered trees and limbs. About a hundred yards ahead, Seikh saw a deep crevice in the ground. "I hope you have a plan to get over that hole in the ground!"

"We aren't going over. We are going *in*!"

"What?"

"Trust me! I know what I'm doing!"

They sprinted toward the crevice. The tar in the pits began to bubble and spew out over the ground. Like small geysers, tar was spouting into the air.

"Hurry! The trees are using the tar in the pits to attack us," Philo yelled as the boiling tar splattered everywhere. Thick, boiling, sticky drops landed on Seikh, burning his skin. Dark streaks of tar streamed down his face, penetrating his flesh with intense heat. Just as they approached the crevice, Philo screamed out. "Jump!"

Seikh dove into the deep ravine.

"Ahhhhh!" Seikh screamed as he held his left leg. Tar was oozing and bubbling down his pants.

"Hold still!" Philo scraped and scratched at the tar in panic with his pack. He ripped his shirt off and furiously wiped Seikh's leg.

A few long moments passed, and Seikh let out a large ghastly sigh. "I think you got most of it."

They were both breathing deeply trying to catch their breath.

"Where's Pseudomai?" Seikh asked while he tore off his charred pant leg, exposing charred hair.

"I don't know. I lost him once the trees attacked us."

"What now?" Seikh spoke with some relief from the pain in his leg.

"Unfortunately, I think we're trapped. There's nowhere for us to go. We could keep running to the east toward the villages, but there are just too many Scarlet Riders. They will just catch up to us. We will have to travel in the ravine to the north as quickly as we can and try to find a place to hide."

"Do you have any other weapons? Any more phanos swords or *anything*?" Seikh's breathing was more settled.

Philo shook his head.

"I wasn't going to say anything . . ." Seikh hesitated. "But since we seem to be in an interesting situation, what about that glass book in your pack? Is it good for anything?"

"I already knew about that. I saw you reading it last night. Do you really think you could have hidden something like that from me?" Philo stared at him seriously. Seikh just stared back.

A moment of silence passed. Philo looked back at Seikh. "So, what did it say?"

"What?"

"The. Book." Philo replied.

"It doesn't matter. It's all foolishness anyway." Seikh shifted and stood up.

"Really? And how do you know that?"

"It doesn't matter! We have Scarlet Riders after us. We have no time for this right now. Can I use that book as a weapon or not?"

"You could try throwing it at them, but I don't think it would do much good," Philo smirked as he wiped his brow.

"Ha, ha." Seikh rejoined.

Philo rubbed his hands together, trying to clean off oil and dirt. He began walking north down the ravine. Seikh followed.

"The only thing that book is good for is reading." Philo jumped over a few large roots that twisted above the ground. "So, what did it say?"

"It said *Zoe* on its front cover." Seikh scaled a few rocks. "What is *Zoe*?"

"That's the book's name."

"The book has a name? I thought books have titles, not names."

"This isn't just any book," Philo replied with some indignation. "It's one of a kind. It tells you about the past, present, and even the future. It tells you what you most need to know." Philo hesitated. "It reveals truth about things to come."

"Truth! Ha!" Just the sound of the word made Seikh angry and feel sick to his stomach. It reminded him of the conversation with Elihu—The Speech, Abaddon, and Lamlorde. Disgust welled up within him. He was on a journey to save his mother, not to find some kind of truth. Seikh blurted out his next immediate thought. "What *is* truth?"

Philo was now walking faster, and Seikh was doing everything he could to keep up the pace. His leg was still throbbing from the tar.

"Well, what did the book tell you?"

"A silly book can't tell me any truth! My truth is my truth, no matter what that book says!"

As these words fell from Seikh's lips, Philo shoved Seikh flat to the ground.

"Someone's coming." Philo's breath fell hard on Seikh's ears. "The Scarlet Riders. They have found us. Listen to me. Whatever happens to us—whatever they do to us—remember what the Book of Zoe told you. It is key to understanding how to find Lamlorde."

"How do you know about Lam—"

Seikh's words were interrupted by the loud clopping of hooves. Philo and Seikh looked up to the top of the ravine. Four horses stood looking down on them—one white, one black, one ashen, and one scarlet. Each horse was saddled by a rider clothed in a robe matching the color of the horse. "Surek's Four Horsemen," Philo muttered.

Philo turned to Seikh. "Remember what I said."

Then Seikh blacked out.

1 2

The Dungeons

Seikh woke up in excruciating pain. The lump on his head throbbed from the blow he received from Surek's Four Horsemen. Something like golden chains clutched his wrists, tying them down to a stone floor. Links were wrapped around his ankles, clenching them tightly. His left leg was still burned from the tar. Seikh opened his eyes slowly. A single light hung above his head, blinding him. He heard a voice that sounded eerily familiar.

"Ah. Yes. This should hold him. Someone in the Infinite is not easy to contain. I am actually impressed that you horsemen were able to subdue him. Good job." The voice came closer to Seikh. "I see he has awoken."

The voice hovered above Seikh's face. Slowly a black pointed hat came into view. Sangoma's long pointed nose punctured Seikh's vision.

"Sangoma . . ." Seikh's voiced trailed off.

"Yes, my boy. I should have known who you were from the beginning. The light of your mind should have made it clear to me. You may have deceived me once, but you will not do it again, *Dreamer*." The derision in Sangoma's voice was obvious. He turned and whisked out of Seikh's sight and began talking to others in the room. "You riders may be excused. Surek is summoning you for your next task."

Footsteps clattered systematically and a door slammed shut with the sound of clanging metal.

Sangoma called out to Seikh. "And you, my boy, will just have to wait here until I find a way to get you to *pass through*, as they say."

Sangoma's voice cackled wildly, and it slowly disappeared. Seikh was left alone on the cold floor.

After moments of attempting to gain some composure, Seikh began to regain his sight. He tried to lift his head, but something restrained it. He shifted his head slowly to the right. Metal bars separated by just a few inches made a wall. Looking up, he saw rock walls surrounding him. He was in a dungeon. Seikh surmised it was Surek's dungeon.

Inhaling as much air as he could, Seikh spoke. "Is. Anyone. There?" Silence. "Hello? Anyone?"

No answer. He could speak no more. His limbs felt light and weak. His eyes closed. He lost consciousness.

A large table that stretched for miles into darkness was surrounded by horrid creatures, the likes of which Seikh had never seen. The creatures ate rancid, spoiled food that was clumped in front of them, and the monsters were yelling and screaming at each other as they chomped and gnashed their teeth. Not one of them took notice of Seikh, who was now standing directly behind one of the tall, backed chairs.

Seikh stood there for what seemed like hours, watching the creatures pridefully devour their food without ever seeming satisfied. The creatures evolved from one type of hideous monster into another.

Crunch. Gnash. Chomp.

The creatures consumed the putrid meat.

What in the world is this?

Seikh's stomach turned, and he recoiled at the sights and smells.

To the right, Seikh caught a glimpse of a large creature with a moose's head. It had the horns of a goat and teeth of a shark. Its claws tore the unsightly flesh strewn on the plate in front of it. It then stopped and stared at the mess. It breathed heavily and then sighed as if catching its breath after a long run. Its shoulders slumped. Its eyes were sad. Slobber dribbled slowly from the corner of its mouth. It lamented in a low voice. "Not the way it's supposed to be." It repeated with its voice trailing lower and softer. "Not the way . . . it's supposed to be."

Seikh was saddened by the creature's words and felt compassion for him. It seemed overwhelmed by helplessness. It was enslaved to a life of eating food that never satisfied.

Seikh lowered his head and tears began to well up. The chair in front of him shifted, and a creature who resembled a donkey was sitting on it. It turned its head and looked seriously and sadly at Seikh. It said nothing. Standing up slowly, it jumped awkwardly onto the table with all four legs coming out from underneath it. Immediately all the creatures dropped their food.

"Treasonous peasant!" yelled out the moose-headed monster. "Grab him! Kill him!"

Chaos ensued. Monsters clutched the donkey's throat and thrust him flat onto the table as it whinnied and yelped. They took knives and slaughtered him.

Seikh's eyes popped open. The dungeon door creaked, and the sound of childish voices filled the dungeon's echoey chamber.

Pravitas.

"I dunno where this delusionary Dreamer goes. Just put him in there. Surek won't care." Chains clamored. The barred door slammed shut. "There! You Dreamer. Hehehe. Let's get some meat."

The Pravitas' voices trailed off and disappeared.

The light that originally shown above Seikh was no longer there. It was dark, except for a dim light coming through a small window about thirty feet up the wall near the ceiling. It was creepy, and the silence was deafening.

"Hello? Is anyone there?"

Seikh looked around. No answer.

A few minutes passed before a low melancholy voice stammered, "If only I had listened. Earlier. Should have. I could have saved my family. Kosmon."

Chains slowly scraped the floor and a figure appeared in the dim light shining through the small dungeon window.

"Hello?" Seikh looked intently at the dark silhouette now standing in the middle of the dungeon. "Who are you?"

The dark shadow did not reply. It slid slowly across the cold hard floor to the other side of the dungeon where a rock set against the wall. The figure sat down with its head lowered and shoulders drooping. It began to sob.

"Hey!" Seikh called out. "Who are you? Talk to me!"

The sobbing began to subside, and the figure lifted its head slowly. "Speech? Is that the sound of The Speech I hear?"

"No, I'm not The Speech! My name is Seikh. Who are you?"

"What?" the voice trembled. "Who's there?" The figure appeared to look anxiously around the dungeon, and then it stood. "Don't play tricks on me! I belong to the great Lamlorde and The Speech, the originator of all. You cannot hurt me. Do what you will. But I have made my commitment known. Here I stand."

"I'm not playing tricks on you. My name is Seikh. I'm a Scientian of Kosmon. Please, tell me where I am."

"Seikh?" the voice queried. "Is that really you?"

The figure stumbled back into the light of the window, its face barely illuminated by the blue hue that filled the air.

Seikh couldn't believe his eyes. "Father?"

"Seikh!" Seikh's father scurried and flung himself to the floor on top of him, arms wrapping tightly around Seikh's body. "My son! My son!" A few moments lapsed and Seikh's father lifted his head from his shoulder and placed his hands on Seikh's face. "You are alive!"

"Of course, I'm alive! But I thought you were dead along with the Dreamers in the Hinnom Meadow. What are you doing here? How did you escape?"

"You were in the Meadow?"

"Yes. I woke up from a dream and heard noises outside, so I snuck out of the house and went to the Meadow. I saw all the Dreamers tied up and you and Mother. They took a vote on whether to put the Dreamers to death and the whole crowd was for it, but for some reason, I spoke out and voted 'no.'"

"That was *you* who voted 'no?'" Seikh's father sat down next to Seikh. He appeared deep in thought.

"Yes, that was me." Seikh said in a somewhat vexed manner. "I'm so sorry, Father. I don't know why I did that. Everything has been a mess since then."

"But *how* did you get there in the first place?"

"I just told you, Father."

"No, Seikh. You don't understand. How could you have gotten there if you were *dead*?"

Seikh gasped. "Dead? What are you talking about?"

"Son, my only son, you died earlier that evening."

"What!" Seikh was stupefied. "What are you talking about? If I died, then how is it that I'm still alive?"

Seikh's father shifted on the cold, solid dungeon floor, stood up, and walked to the wall on the other side of Seikh and sat down. He looked pensive. A few moments of silence passed and Seikh began to get anxious. His father looked intensely at him and spoke earnestly. "There's only one explanation for all this."

Seikh anxiously waited for his father's next words, but he felt as if he knew what was coming. "Seikh, my son. You *did* die. You are now in the Infinite."

The word *Infinite* reverberated in Seikh's head. The message of the Book of Zoe streaked across his mind: *You are in the Infinite. Take courage. The Finite will be overcome. You have been chosen.*

The words of Philo also echoed in his thoughts: *Remember what the Book of Zoe told you. It is key to understanding how to find Lamlorde.*

The string of thoughts all came together and attempted to penetrate his heart. "Father, did I die from the plague the night the Dreamers were killed in the Meadow?"

"Yes, son. You did." Seikh's father stood up slowly. "The night the Dreamers were burned at the stake, the plague took your life. Your mother and I were so distraught. We mourned all evening. The Scientians—and I—had failed to find a cure. Your mother was especially upset, and I did my best to console her, but she couldn't handle losing you. So she went to Surek and convinced him to bring judgment upon the Seers. Surek and his men rounded them all up and held a trial in the Hinnom Meadow. And, as you know, they killed them all. They had been waiting a long time to find a reason to exterminate the remainder of them." He came closer to Seikh and knelt beside him.

Seikh looked deep into his father's eyes. "But how did you escape? They had tied you up and burned you at the stake. I saw it!"

"Evidently you didn't see everything that happened. After they apprehended me, they decided to let me go. I'm Scientian, after all, and not a Seer. The judgment was against the Seers, not anyone else. And so, they decided to arrest me and bring me here to Surek's dungeons to be with the 'delusional people.' They figured that the plague had finally got the best of me." He drew closer to Seikh and placed his hands on his shoulders. "Listen to me, son. When you died, you went from the Finite world of Kosmon to the Infinite. And since I can still see and talk with you now, it must mean

91

that you have been chosen for a special task on behalf of The Speech. That's the only reason why some who go to the Infinite can still be seen and heard in the Finite. You're a Crossover. You must be the chosen one to find Lamlorde, who will bring the cure to Kosmon. The prophecy in the Book of Zoe was right! You are the Seer to rise!"

Seikh became infuriated. "What are you talking about!? You sound like that crazy Dreamer Elihu! And how do you know about the Book of Zoe? It's all a bunch of irrational nonsense! Listen to yourself, Father. What has happened to you? You sound delusional and crazy. Perhaps you *do* belong in Surek's dungeons!"

"No, no, my son! Listen to me! My Scientian ways were wrong. There is more to Kosmon than just the rational, physical world. Lamlorde is real! The Speech is real! If you have spoken to Elihu, then surely you know this all to be true."

"True?" Seikh retorted in disgust. "What is true for me is that I must get out of this dungeon and rescue Mother. She is alive and being held in these dungeons. That's my mission—my meaning and purpose in life. I have reached deep inside myself and have found what is true for me. I know what will make me happy." Seikh paused. "Tolerance. Acceptance."

"What kind of devilish thoughts are those, Son? Happy? What exactly does that mean? Tolerance? Acceptance? For whom? For what? Obviously not for the Dreamers as you call them. They have been slaughtered. Where was tolerance and acceptance then, Son?" Seikh's father stood up furiously. "And as far as truth goes, if something is true, it's not just true for me, but it's true for you—for everyone! And as far as your Mother goes, she's not who you think she is. Where have you gotten such ideas?"

"Where did I get such ideas?" Seikh yelled indignantly. "From you, of course! We Scientians have always relied upon our senses for what is true in this physical world. And as far as meaning goes, we have always relied upon the Transmutant ways of listening to our heart to find happiness."

"Yes, my son." His father's voice was sad. "I taught you that. But it was wrong! I was wrong! As wrong as the plague of Kosmon! Listen to me! Don't be a fool!"

Uncertainty and confusion swirled in Seikh's head. Could everything he was ever taught by his father and mother be wrong? Was Elihu right? And what about Pseudomai? He had been sent from The Speech to direct him to what was really true—to rescue his mother and reestablish his home. To have peace and security. Had Philo been right to be suspicious of Pseudomai?

Seikh's father waffled his hands and knelt again beside Seikh, who was now wriggling inside the golden shackles that chained his wrists and ankles to the floor.

"I beg you, son, listen closely to me. Kosmon is under the rule of a dark spirit named Abaddon. He is using Surek and a necromancer named Sangoma to take control of Kosmon and spread the plague far and wide through his teachings. He wants to eliminate all that is from the Seers—to extinguish all the light. The Scientians have been fooled into thinking that the only rational existence is in this physical world; the Transmutants that they can define themselves and be 'true to who they are.' This is how Abaddon is taking control over Kosmon."

"But this is madness, Father! Surely you have become a Dreamer! You have 'passed through' to the other side!"

"No, Son! I used to think as you do and even taught you those horrid lessons that disparaged the Ancient Order. But you must reject those things now to save Kosmon." He stood, turned, and faced Seikh again. "I have passed through. But only because I see the truth now."

"And when did you 'pass through' to this ideology? Did Elihu get to you?"

"No, Son." Seikh's father stood and began pacing. "I found a book—the Book of Zoe—during my research to find the cure for the plague. It was about a month ago. I had gone to the Kosmonian library to study again the Annals. I wanted to check my historical research again to see if maybe I had missed a clue—*something*—that might lead me to the mystery of the plague."

Seikh was hanging onto every word his father spoke. As the words dropped from his lips, Seikh noticed that his father began to dimly glow pure white.

"It was late, and I headed down into the library's basement. The basement was a mess, disorderly, dusty. Not many are allowed in the basement, not since the teachings of the Ancients had been outlawed. I searched and searched down there to find anything of significance. But there was nothing. I must have been down there for hours. As I began to leave, I switched the lights off. Out of the corner of my eye, I noticed a faint blue hue coming from the far corner. Being curious, I turned the lights back on and meandered toward the blue light. As I approached it, the light got brighter. It was a book made of glass. It said *Zoe* on the front of it. I picked it up and suddenly the book flew open, and pages started turning furiously. It stopped on a page entitled 'The Prophecy and Rise of the Seer.'" Seikh's father began to tremble. "It . . ." he stumbled. "It . . . told of a Seer who would be born of a Scientian and Transmutant. And that he would be chosen at a young age to come before Lamlorde to bring the cure to what plagues Kosmon. He would be chosen to *Seikh* Lamlorde!"

Seikh was confounded and exasperated. He sighed heavily, threw his head up, and cried out, "You *have* gone mad, Father! Reading and then accepting what a crazy book says?"

"Please, Son! You must believe me!"

A voice spoke through the bars of the dungeon. "That is quite enough! Those Pravitas should never have brought you in here together, Dr. Ichabod." Sangoma opened the dungeon door, limping toward them. Four Scarlet Riders followed him. "It's now time to get you to pass through, my little Dreamer. Seikh. It *is* Seikh, isn't it?" Sangoma cackled.

The Scarlet Riders bound him with four red glowing thick chords on the wrists and ankles, unlocked the golden shackles, and led him out of the dungeon. The dungeon door slammed shut and echoed throughout the hall. As the Scarlet Riders began to lead him down the dark, cold hallway, Seikh could hear his father begging him to believe.

"Seikh! Seikh! Take heed to what I said!"

The dim white light that shown from his father melted away into the darkness.

13

The Sultan

The chords that bound Seikh's ankles and wrists were warm and tight, and their red light pierced the darkness of the cold, damp hallway. Two Scarlet Riders led Seikh and two followed him. Sangoma was wobbling down the hall, leading them through narrow doorways, around turns, and past dungeons on either side. As they walked, Seikh attempted to peek into the cells so he could possibly catch a glimpse of who was being held hostage. *Perhaps Mother is being held in one of these dungeons.* But the cells were too dark.

The dungeons were eerily silent. He could not even hear the Scarlet Riders breathing. The clang of a chain or two floated softly through the halls every so often. A scraping of a fork against a plate would echo faintly. No voices could be heard.

Sangoma and the Scarlet Riders stopped. The red chords tightened around Seikh's wrists and ankles, causing him to wince. A large door stood immediately in front of Sangoma. Sounds of numerous locks clicking and chains sliding echoed through the hall. Sangoma bent over and slid up a large lever that was attached to the door. As the lever broke free from the stone floor, the door creaked open. Light pierced the darkness of the hall, blinding Seikh. Sangoma began ascending a stone staircase just on the other side of the heavy, thick door. "C'mon, you riders. Surek wanted to see him right away."

The riders yanked on the red chords, jerking Seikh forward through the large opening and causing him to stumble up the stairs. The staircase was large and had countless steps. As Seikh climbed and tripped over the stairs, his eyes slowly adjusted to the light. Cracked stone walls encased both sides of the staircase. Water seeped slowly through the cracks as if mourning, making Seikh's every step slippery.

The staircase eventually opened up into a large circular room with a dark marble floor and walls of stone. The ceiling was hundreds of feet tall. Large windows lined where the walls met the ceiling. A strong, slithering voice echoed through the spacious room. "Sssangoma! Let thissss lad go."

"But, Surek, the Great Sultan of Kosmon, I found him to be—"

"Sssilence!" interrupted Surek. "Unbind him!"

The four Scarlet Riders dropped the red chords, and they were immediately loosened from Seikh's wrists and ankles. Sangoma collected them.

"You may go. Leave ussss!" demanded Surek.

Sangoma and the riders swiftly disappeared out a door on the left of the room.

"Come clossser, Ssseikh."

Seikh looked around the room and could not discern where the voice was coming from. Then, directly in front of him, Surek emerged from a part of the room which was darkened by shadows. He was dressed in a robe of purple and a golden crown covered with jewels sat upon his head. His face was that of a Scientian. Long locks of dark hair flowed to his shoulder. He did not appear at all as he had in the City of Petra when he and his men killed Elihu.

"Surek?" Seikh looked intently at him, attempting to make sense of his appearance.

"Yesss. It'sss me. Come clossser sssstill."

Surek's lisp was still present, but his appearance was magnificently radiant.

"You look as if you have sssseen ssssomething very sssstrange."

"Uh, no. No. Not at all." Seikh shuffled toward Surek, studying every inch of him along the way.

Surek reached out and took Seikh's hands in his. Surek's palms and long fingers were soft and warm, just like a king's and not a warrior's. "I very much apologizzze for your recent trouble with ssssome of my men. In thisss troubled time, I'm afraid that not everyone can disssscern between the enemiesss of Kosssssmon and itss friendsss. And you, Sssseikh, are certainly itsss friend."

Confused, Seikh ask, "You mean, you are not after me? But at the Hinnom Meadow—"

"Yesss, I know," interrupted Surek. "That wasss a mistake. Sssome of my men occasionally get a little zealousss." Surek let go of Seikh's hands, backing away just a bit to look at him more carefully. The shimmering light from Surek was almost blinding. "But you are one of usss. You are a wissse Scientian. A true citizen of Kosssmon. One who usesss impeccable logic and rationality."

"But what about my mother?"

"What about your mother? She isss quite sssafe."

Surek turned, walked toward his throne, which Seikh had not recognized when he first entered the room, and sat down. The throne shimmered with gold. The back reached many feet above Surek's head.

"Safe?" Seikh queried. "You captured her and are holding her in your dungeons!"

"Oh, Ssseikh! You are quite missstaken. She isss quite well. She isss in no harm. I brought her here to protect her—to keep her sssafe. She proved hersssself at the Hinnom Meadow to be a true Kosssmonian. I would never hurt her—I sssaved her from the unruly mob at the Meadow." Surek looked seriously at Seikh. "In fact, Ssseikh, I have planned to reunite the two of you. That isss what you truly desssire, isn't it? To have things asss they once were?"

Perplexed, Seikh could not answer.

Mother is safe? She doesn't need to be rescued? Surek saved her?

Waiting for a response, Surek breathed deeply and then drank from a golden goblet that had been resting next to his throne. the aroma of wine wafted through the throne room. "You ssseem confused, my boy. Isss there conflict in your mind?"

"I . . . I don't know," Seikh stammered. "I thought—"

"You thought I wasss your enemy?" Surek interrupted.

"Well, yes."

"And the Dreamer Elihu told you storiesss, didn't he? And now you are confused and don't know who to trussst?"

Seikh felt alone and isolated. He hung his head, and his shoulders slumped over. "I just want to know the truth," he spoke softly.

"The truth? Ha!" Surek laughed uncontrollably. After a fit of coughing, he continued, "Ssseikh, my boy, there isss truth in only one thing: what you observe. And what do you obssserve about me? I am the Sssultan of Kosssmon. I have protected your mother and can give you what you mossst desire. You and your mother can ssserve me. I can provide a place for the both of you here in my palaccce. I can provide for your every need. If you will accept."

"But what about Father?"

"Unfortunately, Ssseikh," Surek stroked his long beard, "he hasss become delusional, assss you probably know. He hasss come to believe in the mythsss of the Ssseersss, the Dreamersss." He looked down at the ground, saddened, as if reminiscing of the times he had spent with Father. His face was long. "He wasss one of my bessst men to find the cure." He paused. "And thisss iss why I mussst have you ssserve me. You have the mind of your father, but you are much more rational. You can finish the job he began. You can find the cure for the plague of Kosssmon. I have chosssen *you*. You are ssspecial, Ssseikh."

Suddenly, a door creaked open from behind Surek's throne. A white light appeared with a yellowish hue floating around the edges. A figure walked in wearing all white with a hood.

"Pseudomai?" Seikh spoke in astonishment. "What are you doing here?"

"Pseudomai?" Surek inquired.

"Lucy, what isss the meaning of thisss? I did not sssummon you." He looked embittered and agitated. His eyes glowed red. "And what isss this boy talking about?"

"Lucy?" Puzzled, Seikh looked him over inquisitively, his posture becoming more upright. "Why, you are Pseudomai." He turned and faced Surek, "What are *you* talking about?" He jerked back to Pseudomai. "Lucy?"

"Oh, Seikh." The shining figure drew close to Seikh, took hold of him, and drew his head near its breast. Its touch and warmth were very familiar. Its breathing very soothing. Speaking softly, the figure resembling Pseudomai drawled, "I am Lucy, your mother."

Seikh, gasping, pushed away from her. "No! You can't be! You are Pseudomai."

"No, no, Seikh. I am your mother." The elusive figure slowly pulled down its white hood and the radiant glow slowly dissipated. There was Seikh's mother, a Transmutant, with the horse-like face and long beard hanging from her chin.

Seikh couldn't believe his eyes. "Mother? I . . . I don't understand. You . . ." Anger began to swell inside him. "You lied to me!"

"What isss he talking about, Lucy?" Surek was now standing.

"O Surek, the Great Sultan of Kosmon, I came across my son while returning from my mission to complete the judgment of the Seers. He was being attacked by a pack of gundigans. I saved him from impending death. A mother will always save her son, O Surek. My intention was to bring him here to serve you as I am, but I was unsure he would come with me." She turned toward Seikh. "Oh, my son, I had no intention of hurting you. You were so intent on seeking the mythological character Lamlorde. I had to do something. You had been led astray. You were believing lies. I had to protect you."

"Lies?" Seikh asked vociferously. Resentment filled Seikh. "*You* lied to me! You, my own mother! You have always told me we had a sacred bond of trust—that a bond of trust should never be broken." Seikh breathed heavily and uncontrollably. "Evidently you are much more like the deceptive Seers!"

Seikh's mother slapped his face. "How dare you talk to me that way, Son!" Her voice rumbled and cracked. Her appearance began to change. Her head transformed into a moose head with horns of a goat. A forked snake tongue slithered out between her pointed shark teeth. "You. Will. Serve. Surek. With. Me."

"Mother!" Seikh cried with tears streaming down his face. He fell to his knees. "You . . . You . . ." He couldn't speak. His mother was the creature from his dream who helped slaughter the donkey. Claws protruded from underneath her sleeves, looking as if they would tear into him. "All I ever wanted was to be with you, Mother! To go home. To be happy. But—"

"But what?" Surek interrupted calmly. "Nothing hasss changed here. You are now reunited with your mother. Come. Ssserve me alongssside your mother. Rebuild your heart'sss desssire."

"But she lied to me! She has broken our bond of trust," Seikh trembled uncontrollably. "I have always been a seeker of facts. I may not have always been the best at it—I may have gone astray at times, believing facts to be a creation of my own. But I love facts—just as my father always has, although he may not have been the best at it either. You, however, are full of lies! You almost had me killed! You were helping the Scarlet Riders and the trees. You were helping Sangoma and even the Pravitas! Pseudomai? Nothing but a liar! Philo was right about you—and Father—you are not who you appear to be."

"Oh stop, Seikh! Listen to yourself!" she exclaimed, sounding like a typical, emotionally driven Transmutant. "I saved you from the gundigans!

Sangoma overstepped his orders, and I became your salvation!" She held her arms open wide as if waiting for Seikh to embrace her.

"My salvation?" Seikh replied furiously. Then a thought like a bolt of lightning struck him. "You, Mother, were the Informer, weren't you? You were the one who saw me with Elihu—the one Sangoma spoke of. This has been a trap all along! You have been in league with Surek the whole time!"

Ignoring his comment, Lucy regained her composure, leaned down, and spoke softly into Seikh's ear. "Listen to me, Seikh. You have always been the true rational one." She stroked his cheek carefully and compassionately. "You have always been someone looking for some kind of absolute 'truth.' I've tried to teach you better than that and protect you from the lies of the Dreamers. Oh, Seikh, I am your mother. I would never let anything happen to you. Out of everything in Kosmon, a mother always loves her son above all else."

Seikh looked at her through tears. Painstakingly, he spoke more certainly than he ever had before, "But a son does not always love his mother above all else."

Seikh's mother began to shudder violently, her hand dropping from his face.

"Elihu was right," Seikh continued. "Facts, truth are much more worthy to be loved above all else," Seikh replied confidently. "If I had loved the truth, I would never have been deceived by you."

"Truth? What is truth, Seikh?" Her voice was antagonistic.

"Something you obviously know nothing about," Seikh replied despondently.

Surek began to laugh. "Is thisss how we will ssspend our time? Quibbling over the nature of truth? Sssuch trivialitiesss!"

"It's the only thing that ultimately matters," Seikh retorted.

"It seemsss you have overessstimated your son, Luccccy. It appearsss that he isss in the throesss of the Dreamersss," Surek's voice reverberated venomously throughout the throne room. Turning toward Surek, Seikh now beheld the one who had killed Elihu. Surek's robe was black, and his face obstructed by a draping hood. A snake's tongue protruded from his mouth.

"No, you have *under*estimated me, O Sultan," Seikh countered.

A snake tongue slithered out from Surek's mouth, "You are a Dreamer, young Seikh. You are the one who has bought into liesss. You are delusional!" He turned toward Lucy. "Faith in your ssson hasss failed."

Lucy stood up straight with her eyes penetrating deep into Seikh. A sense of sadness overcame her and then anger and resoluteness.

"He must be bound!" Her voice evinced malice. "He is in the Infinite and is a danger to Kosmon! He will spread the plague if he is ever allowed outside the walls of the castle." She stood alongside Surek. "He is the one foretold by those Dreamers—the Seer born to a Transmutant and Scientian who is to bring back the Ancient Order! I know for I, a Transmutant, am his mother. His father, Dr. Ichabod, is a Scientian. O Surek, Sultan of Kosmon, I adjure you to bind him!"

"Sssangoma!" Surek yelled.

Sangoma and the four Scarlet Riders entered as quickly as they had left earlier. "Yes, Sultan?"

"Bind thisss boy, Ssseikh! Do it quickly. He isss in the Infinite and likely to escape. Take him to the dungeonsss and make sure he never seesss the light of day again."

"Yes, Sultan," Sangoma obediently replied, hobbling toward Seikh and waving his hands, murmuring an incantation. The Scarlet Riders shackled Seikh's wrists and ankles with the same glowing-red chords.

"So, my little Dreamer," Sangoma spoke softly and mockingly in Seikh's ear, "couldn't be *passed through*, huh?" He cackled. "I could have told them you wouldn't turn. There's too much light in your mind. I've seen it too many times over hundreds of years. I knew it was foolish to bring you here to try to win you over. But no worries now. That light will be extinguished."

"You are mistaken, Sangoma. I have passed through—to the side of The Speech and the one who holds the cure, Lamlorde. I am putting my trust in them."

He stood straight, confident.

Grunting in disapprobation, Sangoma pulled on the red chords and handed them to the Scarlet Riders, and they led Seikh to the dungeons.

Part Two

Rise

14

Truth

The Scarlet Riders yanked on the red chords that bound Seikh, pulling him down the stairs that led to the lower dungeons. He lost his balance and tripped down the staircase, cutting his lip on the edge of a stone step. Sangoma grumbled at him, and the riders kicked his sides. Seikh pushed himself up slowly, grasping at anything that he might use to help him stand. The riders pulled on the chords, jerking his arms and hands behind his back, lifting him to his feet.

"Get moving!" shouted one of the riders in a low, disturbing voice.

With every hard step down to the dungeons, Seikh felt like he was closer to death, except he was already dead. What this exactly meant, he did not know. Father, Mother, Sangoma—everyone—knew he was in some other realm known as the Infinite. What was this Infinite? Whatever it was, he had been transferred to it the night he died of the plague, the night the Seers were martyred. Since that mysterious and dreadful event, Seikh had been confused, lost. He had questioned everything and trusted no one— well, almost no one. He had trusted Pseudomai—his mother—and she had deceived him. Seikh had kept his bond of trust with her—he had been faithful. He was going to risk all and rescue her from the hand of Surek. And for what? To find out that his mother had not been captured after all but was leading him to Surek so that he could coopt him for his own plans. Philo had been right: there was something suspicious about Pseudomai.

Seikh put one foot in front of the other, down each step, blood dripping from his lip. He ruminated about Elihu, and he was filled with warmth, light, and peace. How different this was from the coldness, darkness, and turmoil he felt when he had been with Pseudomai and Surek, and those who worked for him. How different he felt now.

As they approached the bottom of the long, descending stairway, the riders stopped in front of the large door that led to the dungeons. Sangoma turned toward Seikh and with eyes wide open, he spoke softly and with amazement. "And what is this?" Sangoma reached out his gnarly fingers, as if to stroke Seikh on his shoulders. "You . . . you are glowing—as pure white. And your mind is filled with light."

Seikh bowed his head. He noticed that his legs and garments were radiating a white hue just like Elihu's had done. The words Seikh had spoken to his mother ricocheted over and over in his head.

Truth must be loved above all else.

He repeated to himself the words he had spoken to Sangoma.

I have passed through.

Seikh could no longer think clearly. The lights of the stairway blinded him. He was weak and emotionally distraught.

I have passed through—to the side of The Speech and the one who holds the cure.

Sangoma, as if reading Seikh's mind, spoke directly to him. "You may have passed through to The Speech and to Lamlorde, his greatness . . ." He stopped. Astonished, Seikh lifted his head and stared into his beady eyes. "Yes, that's right. I know he is no myth."

Sangoma gripped Seikh's chin. "And you may have taken on some of his nature, this eminent glowing, but you will never escape, and you will never find him, so you might as well put it out of your mind. My incantations and chords are impenetrable and will keep you from living the Infinite life. You. Will. Never. Escape."

Sangoma whisked around as if there had been no interruption and began to unlock the numerous locks on the dungeon door.

One lock.

Click!

Two locks.

Click!

Truth must be loved above all else, Seikh thought again.

Three locks.

Click!

Truth must be loved above all else.

Four locks.

Click!

The door creaked open. The darkness from the dungeons reached into Seikh's very soul. The riders tugged the chords on Seikh's wrists, and they entered the black abyss.

The dungeon hallway was as cold and damp as before. An eerie silence still permeated the air. The door slammed shut behind them. The clicking and clanging of locks rang in Seikh's ears.

"Let's take him to the lower cells where he will be isolated from all the others," Sangoma's voice echoed through the corridors.

Light from individual windows inside the cells creeped through the heavy barred doors and cast a bluish hue on the rough stone floor of the hallway. Sangoma and the riders dragged Seikh behind them as they wandered further into the darkness. Seikh wanted to say something, but he didn't know what. He just stared at the sea of blue stones at his feet as he walked painfully between the cells on either side of him.

The hallway was long. Darkness seemed to go on forever. A clanging of a tin can began to be heard in the distance. It sounded like one of the prisoners was slowing rippling it across the bars of a cell. Cling. Clang. Then it would pause. Cling. Clang. Over and over it went.

"What is that?" Sangoma inquired.

"It must be one of the prisoners, sir," a Scarlet Rider answered. "He probably just finished eating the food from his can."

"Take it away from him!" Sangoma said in an irritated manner. "It sounds like it's coming from ahead of us. When we reach him, punish him."

"Yes, sir."

The clanging kept resonating down the hall, and it got louder with every step. Another can began to clang but opposite of the first can. Cling. Clang. Then another can in the distance clanged slowly. Cling. Clang. A faint voice, tired and weak, could be heard saying, "He is here!" More sounds of tin cans began. Soon all the prisoners were banging their cans against the cell bars. A chant ensued among them: "He is here! He is here! He is here!"

"That is enough!" Sangoma yelled furiously. He scurried down the hall, waving his hands and screaming, "Stop! Stop this immediately! That is enough!"

Ignoring Sangoma, some of the prisoners began to chant more loudly, "The chosen one! The chosen one!"

The voices raised to shouts. The ruckus was overwhelming and Seikh became disoriented.

What are they yelling about?

He fell to his knees and covered his ears. As he collapsed, he noticed that the bright white aura was still about him, gleaming through the hall. The prisoners in the cells next to him appeared and they began chanting, "He is here. He is here," looking right at him. Seikh slowly dropped his hands from his ears. The chanting resounded in his ears like thunder. He lifted his head, stood, and looked at the prisoner to his right.

"The chosen one! The chosen one!" he yelled. Seikh stood still, quietly facing him. "The chosen one! The chosen one!"

Without warning, a voice of tremendous power penetrated the dungeons. "Silence!" The prisoners immediately dropped their cans and fell to the ground, and Seikh with them. A green fog filled the air, taking Seikh's breath away. Sangoma was levitating through the hall. As he came nearer to Seikh, he descended back to the dungeon floor. "That is quite enough," he said calmly. "Riders, get this 'enlightened one' down to isolation away from these disgusting, filthy Dreamers. I will stay here to teach these mythers a lesson."

The Scarlet Riders pulled Seikh to his feet and began dragging him swiftly down the hall, causing Seikh to stumble and fall, scraping his knees and jamming his shoulder into the ground. The riders dragged him by his wrists and ankles to the door at the end of the hallway. Chains that kept the door locked fell, and the door swung open without any assistance. The riders pulled Seikh through the doorway, slamming his head into the edge of the door. They began descending another stairway, but this time it spiraled downward. Seikh tried to stand, but the riders were pulling him too quickly and with such a force that he could not get loose from the torturous fall down the stairs. Seikh bumped his head and his ribs slammed into the steps, over and over.

"Stop! Let me up!" Seikh hollered repeatedly.

The riders came to a stop at the end of the stairs. The four of them stood there staring at Seikh.

"Get up!" one stated, forcing his wrists and arms above his head. Out of breath, bruised, and bleeding, Seikh slowly stood up. Darkness surrounded them, except for a torch hanging on the wall, just to the right of another large door. The riders nudged him and then thrust his body toward the door. One of the riders grasped the torch and removed a large steel lever that kept the door sealed. The door slowly opened and sucked air as it swung on its hinges. It was at least six inches thick. The rider with the torch floated through the doorway and the other three pulled Seikh through it.

The hall they entered was completely dark. No windows allowed any light in. Only the torch and Seikh's glimmer of white light trickled upon the bars of the dungeon and the floor. Drips of water could be heard in the distance. The riders continued their march, yanking the chords around Seikh's wrists and ankles. The hallway was narrow and short. They halted after walking a few steps.

"This is complete isolation," one rider spoke gruffly. "You will have no companionship. You will have no way out." He opened a cell door and walked in, drawing Seikh into a small, musty cell that was similar in size to the cell Seikh had been in originally. The four riders began weaving the red chords that shackled Seikh through steel hoops attached to the floor.

Suddenly, a voice spoke in the darkness. "Except you have made an error in judgment."

"What did you say?" The Scarlet Riders looked at Seikh.

"I didn't say anything," replied Seikh, looking about the darkness.

The riders' eyes meandered around the dungeon, looking for the voice that had spoken.

"But I did," said the voice. A yellow light from a phanos sword lit up the cell, piercing the darkness. "You made the error of not expecting me!"

Philo then thrust his sword, stabbing one of the Scarlet Riders through the chest. He fell to the stone floor and disappeared. With expert swiftness, Philo wielded his sword, swiping at two of the three remaining riders, slicing them in half and making them disintegrate. The final rider had pulled out a knife that glowed red. Philo did a half turn and his sword collided with the red rider's weapon with a shattering sound that echoed throughout the dungeon. The red rider pulled back, swiping at Philo's head. Philo ducked, plunging his sword toward the rider's stomach. The rider stepped back and then lunged at him. By this time, Seikh was behind the rider, and he wrapped his chords around the rider's neck, pulling as hard as he could, strangling him. Philo, with a yell and a vigorous, precise thrust of his sword, buried his phanos blade into the rider's chest. The rider evaporated like the others, leaving Seikh and Philo in the cell alone.

Philo cut through the red chords that gripped Seikh's wrists and ankles. Orange and red sparks lit the air as the chords fell to the ground. Philo dropped his sword to his side. Breathing heavily, he spoke to Seikh.

"Now, let's find a way out of here." Philo said as he turned and began making his way out the cell door.

"Wait! How did you get here? *Why* are you here?" Seikh asked.

"For one thing, I am in the Infinite just like you now. Living in the Infinite gives one uncanny abilities."

"But how? I thought you had been taken captive just like I was when we fell into the ravine."

"No, not at all. You blacked out when one of the four horsemen struck you with his rod. In his very next move, he killed me."

"So then why did you come to rescue me?" Seikh blurted out.

"Because you are the chosen one." He threw Seikh the phanos sword. "Aren't you?"

Seikh gripped the sword and smiled. "Well, I guess," he spoke hesitantly but almost in awe.

"Then let's do what Elihu commanded you. Let's find Lamlorde."

Seikh and Philo made their way back to the spiral staircase. As they began to ascend it, Sangoma's voice floated down from the top of the stairs.

"What do we do?" Seikh whispered to Philo.

"We hide." Philo pulled Seikh by the arm, swiftly making his way toward the bottom of the stairs. A small wooden door was nestled in the stone wall just beneath the staircase. Philo pulled on its handle. "Get in!"

Seikh scurried through the doorway and entered a dark small room just big enough for the both of them. Philo gently closed the door behind them.

"How are we going to hide with this light emanating from me?" Seikh questioned.

"No worries. Like I said, living in the Infinite gives us uncanny abilities," Philo replied.

Sangoma's footsteps were heard above them as he descended the stairs. He was mumbling something under his breath. Then it was silent. The shuffling of feet could be heard, and then words of paranoia. "What? Where did they go? No! This can't be!"

In the small dark room, Philo spoke softly. "Take my hand."

"What?"

"Trust me. I know what I'm doing."

Seikh grasped Philo's hand. He noticed that the light that emanated from him was getting dimmer.

"Now close your eyes and focus on the light that is coming from you."

Seikh closed his eyes and emptied his mind of everything but his light. He felt warm, pure, and light as a feather, and then as if he were melting. With his eyes closed, he could see through the wooden door and the walls around them. He saw Sangoma on the other side of the door, facing them. He was speaking an incantation. When he finished, the door opened slowly.

"Where are you?" Sangoma spoke softly and inquisitively. His beady eyes seemed to look right through Seikh.

"What's happening?" Seikh asked softly. "Can't he see us?"

"No. He can't see or hear us. We are in the Infinite, and so we are imperceptible to him. This is one of the abilities we gained when we passed through and entered the Infinite. We can both perceive and interact in the physical world and the nonphysical world. But the physical world cannot always perceive us. One must have eyes to see in order to perceive into the Infinite."

Sangoma entered the tiny dark room and looked intently. "I'd swear that my senses tell me someone or something is here . . ." His words trailed off as he searched every corner of their hiding place.

Philo turned toward Seikh and spoke calmly. "Do you remember when you and Pseudomai found me in your house? I don't know if you noticed, but at first, I couldn't see him. He was invisible to me. This is why I knew something was not right with him. He must have been in the Infinite, hiding himself. But when you introduced him to me, he must have made himself visible, and then I saw him. Pseudomai must also be dead and now living in the Infinite."

It all made sense now to Seikh. Pseudomai, whom he now knew was his mother, really had been killed in the Hinnom Meadow. This explained her white luminescence, uncanny abilities, and weapons. Everything she had done was accomplished to deceive him.

"Well, you were right. Something *was* suspicious about him, or I should say *her*. She is my mother, and she is working for Surek."

"That makes things complicated," Philo replied matter-of-factly.

Sangoma finished his search of the little room and began climbing the stairs. He paused, looking down the staircase.

"Is he even *able* to see us?" Seikh asked.

"I don't know. He may be able to use dark powers to see us if he suspects something."

"Let's hope he doesn't."

"I don't think hope is going to help us now."

Sangoma began waving his hands. "If you are here, I will see you."

"Got any ideas?" Seikh began to tremble. "I think he's going to be able to see us very soon if we don't get out of here somehow."

"I'm new at living in the Infinite, but let's try a trick I know about." Philo postured himself near Seikh, who was still holding his hand. "With your eyes still closed, envision the front of this castle."

"I've never seen the outside of this castle, so how am I supposed to do that?"

"Well, just envision something about this castle."

"Okay."

Seikh shut his eyes tightly. The first picture that came to his mind was the dungeon he had been in with his father. In an instant and with a flash of light, Seikh and Philo found themselves in the cell with Seikh's father.

15

Escape

Seikh's father jumped and toppled to the cold, hard, stone floor. "Don't hurt me! Please!" He scooted back and cowered into a dark corner of his cell.

"We aren't going to hurt you," Philo spoke gently.

"How can he see us? Aren't we in the Infinite?" Seikh inquired.

Seikh's father looked more closely at them, "Son? Is that you?"

Philo, somewhat amazed, answered Seikh, "He evidently has eyes to see. He must have passed through." Philo turned to Seikh's father. "Dr. Ichabod? Have you passed through? Do you serve The Speech and the great servant Lamlorde?"

Dr. Ichabod coughed, clearing his throat. "Yes. Yes, I serve the Great Speech. Who are you and how did you get here?"

"I am Philo, your son's friend. We don't have time to explain everything right now. We must leave before Sangoma and Surek's men find us."

"Father!" Seikh stepped forward and placed his hands on his father's arms. "You must come with us. If you serve The Speech, you must help us find Lamlorde and bring an end to the plague."

"Oh, Son!" Father exclaimed. "You have come to your senses! You have listened!" He was overwhelmed with joy, his face beaming. "I will come with you under one condition. We must set all the prisoners free who are being held captive here by Surek. They, too, can help us."

"We can't," retorted Philo. "We don't have time. Besides, the more people who come with us the more difficult the journey will be. We must stay as hidden as possible."

"Philo's right, Father. There will be another time we can come back and set the captives free. We must focus upon the task The Speech has given us."

Father looked down. "I suppose you are right. What's the plan to get out of here?"

Looking at Philo, Seikh spoke, "How about the same way we came—using the powers we have by being in the Infinite?"

"Won't work," Philo responded. "Although your father has passed through, he is capable of only living in the Finite. He cannot travel as we do. We will have to make a run for it as if we are still living in the Finite so we can all stick together."

"Well, I do have this." Seikh held out the phanos sword and the blade came to life, shining yellow and red. "Surely this will come in handy."

"Ahh!" Seikh's father expressed with great emotion, his eyes lighting up and twinkling. "A phanos sword! A great weapon indeed, and to be wielded by the chosen one! Where did you get this?"

"It should look familiar to you, Dr. Ichabod," responded Philo, "I took it from your house, along with the Book of Zoe."

Seikh and his father looked at Philo in shock as Seikh sheathed his sword. "You what?" asked Seikh.

"There's no time for a lengthy explanation now. Just know that before you and Pseudomai showed up, Seikh, I found the book and the sword at your house. That's what I was doing there. I think that's why your house had been broken into—Surek's men came to look for the sword and the book."

"Why would they want the sword and the book?" Seikh queried.

"Because whoever wields the sword is the chosen one and if he doesn't have it, then he cannot accomplish his task"

Seikh stroked the phanos sword at his side. *The chosen one*, he thought, *has it now*.

"And the book," interjected Dr. Ichabod, "because it has the prophecies in it and sheds light on how to find Lamlorde. Where is the Book of Zoe now?"

"I bet Surek has it." Philo said pensively. "It was in my pack when the four riders killed me. I assume they took it and gave it to Surek."

"Then we must find it! It will be of great help as we seek Lamlorde."

"But how?" Seikh looked at his father in distress. "We can't just go wandering around the castle. We have got to get out of here before Sangoma finds us."

"Son, settle down!" Dr. Ichabod braced Seikh with his hands. "The Speech will protect us. There is nothing to fear. It is imperative that we get our hands on that book so we can find Lamlorde."

"It sounds like you're quite familiar with this book," Philo commented.

"I've read the whole thing." Dr. Ichabod's voice was soft and raspy. "It's what persuaded me to pass through to The Speech."

"Then we must get it as quickly as possible and get out of here." Philo turned with a whisk and began toward the dungeon door. "Seikh, use the sword to cut us out of here."

Seikh hesitated. He had never used this kind of sword. He unsheathed it slowly. It lit, and the yellow and red light pierced the darkness. Wielding it rather clumsily, he cut the lock off the cell door, flinging it open wide.

Philo led Seikh and his father down the long hallway toward the large door that led into Surek's throne room. Philo spoke with haste, "We will search Surek's throne room for the book first. This is the most logical place to begin."

"What if Surek is there?" asked Seikh.

"It's a chance we'll have to take."

"I agree," Dr. Ichabod inserted. "You have that sword for a reason, Son. Use it if you have to." Seikh's face filled with concern. "Don't worry about me, Son. Because I have eyes to see, I have a few abilities, although I still live in the Finite."

Suddenly, footsteps began echoing down the dungeon hall and voices filled the air.

"Sheath your sword, Seikh!" Philo anxiously pressed.

Immediately, Seikh put the sword to his side, making the light go out. Except for a small amount of blue light filtering through a few windows from the cells, darkness surrounded them. Even Seikh's aura was no longer visible.

"Now what do we do?" Seikh's voice was barely audible. "We need to get through this door, and I cannot use my sword without them seeing us."

"Shh!" Dr. Ichabod gently pushed Seikh to the side. "Luckily, this door is made of wood and not steel or stone." With those words, Dr. Ichabod walked through the door like a phantasm.

"How in the world did he do that?" Seikh stared at the door with his eyes wide.

"That must be what he meant by 'abilities,'" Philo replied.

The locks on the door began to turn slowly, one right after another, from the other side of the door. Then with a small creak, the door was nudged open, letting a small sliver of light into the hallway.

"We are going to have to make this quick." Philo was crouched near the ground with Seikh right behind him. "On the count of three, I'll open the door and we'll run through. We'll have to shut it quickly and then lock it before the riders and whoever else is down there can reach us."

Seikh could feel his heart pounding in his rib cage, and he bit his lip. "Then, we'll have to search the throne room quickly for the book."

"Ready?" Philo asked.

"Ready."

"One . . ."

"Hey!" a voiced yelled from the other end of the hall.

"They've spotted us. Let's go!" Seikh pushed Philo from behind while Philo swiftly opened the door and slid through along with Seikh. Seikh then slammed the door and began turning locks as fast as he could.

Philo tapped Seikh on the shoulder. "You know what?"

"What?" Seikh replied as he finished latching the final lock.

"We really need to get used to living in the Infinite. We didn't need to do that at all. We could have floated through the door just like your father."

Seikh looked at Philo, rolled his eyes, and spoke in disgust. "Well, no worrying about it now. Let's start looking for the book before they get here."

"I already have it!" Dr. Ichabod's voice echoed softly through Surek's darkened throne room.

Seikh and Philo looked up, and at the top of the stairway was Dr. Ichabod, holding the luminescent, glass Book of Zoe.

"How did you find it so fast?" Seikh asked.

"It's easy to find something that glows in the dark and calls out your name."

"It talks to you, too, huh?" Seikh replied.

"Evidently. Now let's get out of here."

He turned and scurried to the far side of the room. Philo and Seikh, running up the stairs, followed close behind him.

They scampered through a doorway that led into a long, narrow, dark hallway.

"I assume you know how to get out of this castle?" Seikh asked, breathing much harder now.

"I'm assuming the same thing," his father replied with some confidence. "I plan on getting out of here the same way I came."

He abruptly turned left and dashed through a doorway that led them into a large dining hall. Seikh suddenly stopped. He couldn't believe his eyes—a long narrow table sat in the middle of the room adorned with a white cloth and surrounded by tall thin chairs.

"What's wrong?" Philo asked anxiously. "We can't stop. We gotta keep moving!"

"This dining hall. I've seen it before."

"You've seen it before?" asked Dr. Ichabod. "How could you?"

Seikh just stared at the table. "In my dreams."

Suddenly voices could be heard from the hall.

"You will have to tell us about it later. We need to go." Dr. Ichabod replied as he and Philo turned and ran.

"C'mon!" Philo called out.

Seikh took off and caught up with them. They turned right and passed through a doorway at the end of the dining hall, and they found themselves sprinting down another long corridor. Both sides of the hall were lined with bronze statues of soldiers in armor, standing at attention with battle axes.

"Wait a minute!" Philo stopped and placed his hands on Seikh and his father. "Look up. The ventilation system. We can escape through it."

Seikh looked up to the ceiling and saw a barely noticeable large, square iron grate. Right underneath it was one of the statues. He quickly began climbing the statue, then reached out and grasped the grate with both hands, yanking it with as much force as he could. It pulled loose with a small clank.

"Up we go!" announced Seikh as he slid the grate up into the ventilation shaft.

As Seikh pulled himself up through the opening, Philo and Dr. Ichabod whispered for him to hurry. "They're coming!"

Philo was next to go through the opening. Once situated, Philo offered his hands to help Dr. Ichabod climb up.

"Can you make it?" Philo called down.

"Yes. I'm just not as small as I once was." With a grunt and with Seikh and Philo's help, Dr. Ichabod pulled himself through the opening, scraping the sides of his wide frame. "I don't desire to do that again," Dr. Ichabod exhaled, noticeably out of breath, and he rubbed his backside. "That battle ax wasn't very helpful either."

Seikh pulled the iron grate over the opening and secured it. Philo took the lead again. "Follow me! But stay low. The ventilation shaft is not very tall."

Crawling on their hands and knees, they took off straight down the shaft. After several minutes, Seikh's hands and knees were in excruciating pain.

"How much further do we have?" he asked in exasperation.

"Probably another fifteen or twenty minutes. This shaft will take us to the rear of the castle. From there we will be able to climb down Black Mountain and get on our way to Lamlorde."

Somewhat breathlessly, Dr. Ichabod cried out, "But where will this shaft take us? We'll still be in the castle, so how will we get out?"

"I'm hoping," replied Philo, "the shaft will have an opening in the back hall. And since we have abilities, as you say, we should be able to float right through the back doors."

"That sounds like a good plan to me," Seikh replied.

"Wait a minute! Stop!" Philo held his hand up. "I hear someone below us."

Seikh pressed his ear to the bottom of the ventilation shaft. He heard a voice, and then another. There were at least two people below them. He listened intently to discern what was being said.

"Sangoma! Sangoma! How did you lose them? You have been the necromancer for the kings of Kosmon for how long, and you still cannot keep hold of a prisoner? Your powers are not as strong as you think they are! You are getting old!"

"Don't question my powers, my king! There is nothing wrong with my powers. He had help escaping—powerful help! It must have been The Speech or even Lamlorde himself."

"Huh!" King Surek led out a loud grunt. "You believe in these mythological stories and figures? You are dumber than I thought."

"You may believe what you want to believe. But my beliefs are my own, so don't question them." Sangoma sounded disgusted. "Besides, we still have hope if my powers cannot lead us to the boy. We still have the Informer. He is out there somewhere looking for him."

"Yes. Indeed." Surek's voice calmed. "Can we trust him?"

"Most definitely. The Informer knows everything about Seikh. He will find him."

"Good. We must not allow any dissent in my kingdom."

"Ah. There won't be, Great Sultan of Kosmon!"

Footsteps lingered and then silence fell over the room below them. Seikh lifted his head from the shaft.

"Did you guys hear that?" Seikh whispered.

"No. I couldn't hear anything," Philo responded.

In a muffled voice, Seikh recounted the conversation, and then began to tremble. "They are looking specifically for me."

"It's because you are the chosen one," Seikh's father replied. "Sangoma knows the power you could wield if you reach Lamlorde. And Surek, well, he thinks all this is nothing but myth. He just doesn't want to lose his power, and you're a threat to it. You have shown yourself to be an independent thinker."

"If this is the case, then we must be diligent to hurry. We must find Lamlorde as quickly as possible," interjected Philo. "Let's move!"

They all began crawling, quietly yet swiftly. No more than ten minutes passed, and Philo paused.

"Here's an iron grate. I can see down. It looks like we're in another hallway. Yes! We are!" he commented with great joy. "And we are right at the back doors."

Philo tugged at the grate and easily lifted it up. He poked his head down through the hole and came back up. "It's all clear."

Philo jumped down through the opening with Seikh following him. Once in the hallway, Seikh stood beneath the opening to allow his father to use him as a ladder. He came down with a slight thud on Seikh's shoulders, crushing him to the floor. Out of breath, Seikh lay flat on the floor, moaning.

"Sorry, Son!"

"No problem, Father." Seikh, still breathless, slowly rose to his feet.

"Are you guys ready to float through this door?" Philo asked.

"I suppose. As long as I don't need any oxygen," Seikh commented.

Without missing a step, Dr. Ichabod just walked right through the door.

"Now our turn." Philo grabbled a hold of Seikh's hand. "Now think of the backside of this door, and that's where we'll end up."

Gripping Philo's hand tightly, Seikh closed his eyes, thought of the backside of the door, and walked forward with Philo. When he opened his eyes, they were outside the castle, looking at his father, who had a wearied look on his face. "We have a little descent to make to get off this mountain," he commented, cocking his head and gazing down a steep cliff.

Seikh peered over the edge. "What are those?"

About fifty feet below stood some wooden contraptions.

Philo peeked. "Those are trebuchets. I could recognize those anywhere."

"Trebuchets? Why does Surek need those weapons?" Seikh inquired.

"There's only one reason why a king would have trebuchets," Dr. Ichabod retorted. "War."

"War? Who's at war?" Seikh asked.

"It's not 'who's at war?' It's 'who is going to declare war?'" Dr. Ichabod stroked the hair on top of his head.

Seikh craned his head toward his father. "Declare war? Surek wouldn't dare do that."

"No?" interjected Dr. Ichabod. "And why not? The prophecy of the chosen one—you—is coming to fulfillment, and his time is short."

"But Surek doesn't believe in the myths of the Ancient Order," Seikh stated, confused.

"No, he doesn't," Seikh's father affirmed. "He thinks they're fairy-tales—irrational myths made up by the Seers to control Kosmonians and take control of Kosmon. In reality, Surek is just a pawn of Abaddon who desires to exterminate the Seers, and everything related to the Ancient Order. Abaddon wants to maintain rule of Kosmon, and he's using Surek to do it. Having Surek declare war on the Seers and anyone who dares to tell stories of the Ancient Order is how Abaddon will attempt to accomplish his will. And let us not forget about Sangoma. He knows the truth about Lamlorde and the Ancient Order: he knows it's all true. He will just be used by Abaddon to whisper his directives into Surek's ears. In fact, I have a hunch that Sangoma is really Abaddon's servant."

"If this is true, then we must find Lamlorde more quickly than we thought." Urgency filled Seikh's voice. "We must travel day and night until we reach the Woods of Ivory."

"Of course, we should," Philo said proudly and boldly. "But we must use the Book of Zoe to help us find the exact location of Lamlorde. Once we get far away from Surek's castle, we ought to consult it."

"I agree," Dr. Ichabod answered. "Lead on, Philo. You helped us escape. Take us down this mountain and get us to safety."

16

The Journey

Seikh watched Philo as he bounded down the mountain, but then faltered to the ground. He rolled down the side of the mountain before stopping himself just short of a trebuchet. Seikh and his father followed down the incline as if racing to save their lives. Both had lost their balance when their feet slipped on some loose rocks.

Lying on the ground, moaning in pain, Seikh managed to catch a glimpse of Philo, who was pushing himself up from the ground and then called out to him and his father. "Is everyone alright?" Philo's voice echoed from about thirty yards away.

"Yes!" Seikh called back as he lifted himself from the ground, brushing off his clothes. Turning to his father, he held out his hand and helped him up. "Is the book safe?"

"Yes. It's still in tact, fortunately" he replied, almost out of breath. He lifted the book in his hands and then commented hesitantly. "Well, except for this scratch I suppose. Why does it have to be made out of glass?"

"At least it isn't broken." Seikh looked around. "We need to find something to pack that book in—to protect it as well as keep it hidden. I wish I still had my backpack."

"This will work," Philo interjected, walking toward them. In his hand he held an old, ragged, brown knapsack. "I found it hanging on the trebuchet over there."

Dr. Ichabod grabbed hold of the knapsack and untied its strings. Peering inside, he whistled. "And what do we have here?"

He pulled out what looked like a handle to a whip. It was bronze with studded grips.

"Why that's a laser whip—the choice weapon of Surek's men," Philo responded, stepping closer and gazing at it.

"What's it doing out here?" Seikh questioned.

"It must have been left by accident," Seikh's father said, sounding puzzled. He looked around at the sea of trebuchets that lined the grassy plain. "It seems to me that Surek's men must be using forced labor to build these trebuchets, hence the whip—to keep the workers in line."

"I bet Surek is forcing the prisoners in the dungeons to build these," Seikh replied.

"Yes, most likely, or he uses it for some other evil purpose," Philo responded, now gripping the whip and looking it over, and then handing it back to Dr. Ichabod.

"Then this means we *must* do something to free them," Seikh emphatically stated, eyes wide open. "We can't leave them here."

"We will, Son," replied Seikh's father. "But remember: we must get to Lamlorde first. Only he will be able to help us. We are powerless against the dark forces of Surek, and especially Sangoma, without him. The enemy wants to distract us, but we must keep our focus." He placed the whip inside his cloak. "Now, come. Let's get out of here. Our journey will be difficult. We have to go all the way around Black Mountain and make our way to the Woods of Ivory."

Dr. Ichabod turned and wove his way between the trebuchets as fast as he could. Seikh and Philo followed close behind. Seikh turned for a moment and gazed at Surek's castle embedded in Black Mountain. Numerous towers and turrets lined the mountain's landscape. The gray and ominous clouds above seemed to act like a suffocating blanket laying on the castle's roof, taking away all life within. The darkened windows kept any light from escaping or anyone from looking inside. Small chimneys peppered much of the castle's roofline, smoke floating toward the sky and mixing with the clouds.

Seikh turned back around, focusing his eyes on the back of his father's head.

Surely there must be a quicker way to the other side of this mountain.

"Wait!" Seikh yelled out, tugging on his father's shoulder and pressing Philo to a halt. "Isn't there a path that leads around the mountain on the north side? Isn't that what you told us, Philo? Remember when we were with Pseud—" Seikh felt a pit in his stomach and then corrected his next word, "my mother?"

He barely got the word out. He felt disgusted that his mother had become a pawn of Surek.

"It's alright, Son." Seikh's father took hold of his arm. "Mother has chosen her path, but there's always hope that she may turn back to the truth."

His father's words had a sense of hope in them. *Perhaps,* Seikh thought. *Perhaps.*

"Philo, you mentioned that you recalled seeing a side path when you visited with your school class."

"Yes, Seikh," Philo replied. "There is a path to the north of the castle. But remember: it's heavily guarded."

With his thoughts still dwelling on his mother, Seikh replied, "But if we could figure out a way to get through, it would be much shorter."

"And quicker!" Dr. Ichabod exclaimed, letting go of Seikh's arm. "We don't have a lot of time. With as many trebuchets as Surek has already completed, I'm sure he will be planning his attack on Kosmon sooner than later."

"I think you're correct," Philo said contemplatively. "Then I must come up with a plan." He turned to the castle, investigating it. A few silent moments passed. "There!" Philo announced, pointing to the north end of the castle. "Just to the left of those large black boulders. Do you see that gray streak? That must be the path. It looks like it winds up and around the mountain."

"It looks like trees are lining it," Seikh replied, squinting. "Maybe we can just follow the path while hiding in the trees rather than actually taking the path itself? That way we can stay hidden."

"That's a marvelous idea, Son," Dr. Ichabod retorted, patting Seikh on the back. "But get ready for an arduous climb to get up there."

"I'll gird my loins," Seikh said, smirking.

"Here, Father. Take this." Seikh handed Dr. Ichabod a solid branch he had broken off a tree. "You can use this as a walking stick."

"Thank you!" Dr. Ichabod accepted it with a grateful look.

Dr. Ichabod was already showing clear signs of exhaustion and they had not even made it halfway up the mountainside. The rocky incline made the climb arduous for the three of them, but especially for Dr. Ichabod. His usual limp had turned into a wobble and a hop. The thirty-year-old injury to his hip was getting the best of him. Seikh wondered if his father was going to be able to make it. But his father never complained about any pain and did not let on to losing any strength. He never did, not even when Seikh was younger. He just kept plowing forward.

"How do you do it, Father?"

"Do what?" he responded innocently.

"Keep on climbing? Keep walking? You've had that hip injury for as long as I can remember, and you just keep going. Does it ever hurt?"

"Of course," he responded with no despondency. "All the time."

"But you never complain about it."

"Oh, I used to—many times. Your mother would get rather upset with me always talking about it," he commented rather nonchalantly, stepping over some rocks in his path and then pausing to look up at the trees that hovered over them. He inhaled deeply and sighed.

"What happened? What made you stop complaining?" Seikh stood beside his father, staring at him with inquisitive and admiring eyes.

"Well, there comes a point in life that you realize there is no use in complaining about the pain you experience." He looked down at his hip and rubbed it, and then looked straight at Seikh like he was about to tell him something important. "And," his voice softened, "just maybe a thorn in the flesh is given to us to teach us something. Maybe humility, or love, or compassion, even empathy." He began to stir some dirt at his feet with the butt of his newly acquired walking stick. "And maybe to form us into something . . . something better."

Seikh caught a glimpse of Philo out of the corner of his eye. He had stopped just a few yards further up the incline, and Seikh could tell he was now listening to their conversation.

"And to think," Philo piped up, sounding somewhat arrogant, "I thought pain and evil in this world was due to happenstance—bad luck."

"Huh!" Dr. Ichabod grunted. "I once thought that, too—when I was a confounded rationalist, believing everything in this world of ours operated according to immutable laws of cause-and-effect that determined our destinies."

"And now?" Philo questioned.

"I see more clearly. Everything certainly occurs for a reason, but not because it is all determined by the colliding of nonthinking material, but because The Speech either wills it or allows it. Either way, The Speech has his reasons. He has his plans and even hijacks our evil deeds for his purposes. Nothing is left to its own devices, although we all have our own choices to make."

Seikh shifted his feet uncomfortably. "You mean The Speech is controlling everything in this world? If that's the case, then how do we have any choice in the matter? Why are we doing anything? Why not just give it all up to fate?"

"Don't misunderstand me, Son. The Speech doesn't control Kosmon in the way you are using that word. The Speech is certainly in control, but he does not control us and everything in Kosmon like puppets on a string. No, no. Not at all. Like I said, he allows you to make your choices, but don't expect him to sit idly by if he can use your foolish deeds for his plans. That's just how The Speech is: he uses everything for his purposes, one way or another." He stretched out his arms and began to chuckle, "Why, look at me. I'm one of the most foolish fellows of all history! But here I am, here *we* are, somehow in the plan for searching for Lamlorde. And you, Seikh, chosen to lead the way. Our paths have not crossed by mistake, but by the will of The Speech."

"Well, this is all very interesting," Philo interjected, looking bored and impatient, "but we really ought to keep moving."

"Ah, yes. You are right, Philo." Dr. Ichabod trudged up the incline. "But I am a little surprised that you do not know about some of this wisdom. You seem to know quite a bit about passing through and living in the Infinite. This has not been revealed to you yet?"

"Well, I suppose we all have a little more to learn. I will never be omniscient, after all." Philo smirked and then turned to continue his way up the mountain.

"You have spoken truly, Philo. 'Tis true. We all have much to learn," Dr. Ichabod observed, hiking unsteadily past Philo and taking the lead slowly up the mountainside.

Seikh followed closely behind, thinking deeply.

All of Kosmon being orchestrated by The Speech? How mysterious! How marvelous! How comforting! If The Speech is truly orchestrating all of reality, then there is no way he—we—can lose. Abaddon will most certainly be destroyed. Surek and Sangoma—all the forces of darkness will be conquered.

Seikh began to feel a sense of confidence and peace. Confidence because, ultimately, the success of finding Lamlorde did not depend entirely upon his own power but The Speech's. Peace because all he had to do was focus on the task given to him and exercise his will wisely and use it for good. Sure, he might fail or make poor decisions, but somehow The Speech would coordinate it all to bring victory to Kosmon, to bring the cure for the plague, and to restore it to what it once was. Philo, his father, and he were working *with* The Speech to bring the cure to Kosmon. Seikh's next thought was frightening, yet exciting.

We are going to be co-creators of a restored Kosmon!

"Seikh!" Philo called out, interrupting his thoughts. "Wake up! Are you dreaming again? Get over here!"

Seikh looked up from the ground and located Philo and his father scurrying behind some brush beside some large trees. He quickly ran, joining them.

"Get down!" whispered Philo emphatically.

Peering through the brush and around the trees, Seikh saw two Scarlet Riders trotting on horseback, carrying javelins that glistened in a few rays of sunlight that had peeked through the treetops. Having been so deep in thought, Seikh had not noticed the sunbeams. It was odd. The sun had not shone for years. The last time he remembered seeing sunlight was when he was a little boy. The sight of golden yellow streaks through the treetops brought a sense of warmth. The Scarlet Riders noticed the sun immediately and came to a halt. Their horses stood deathly still. Vines and branches cluttered a fence that separated the path that led to the castle's dungeons and the thick wooded forest that Philo, Dr. Ichabod, and Seikh were traipsing through.

"What is this?" one of the riders asked, turning to the other and looking mystified at the sunbeams that danced upon the dark glove that encased his right hand.

"Sunlight!" the other exclaimed.

"What does it mean?" the first inquired, his hands gripping the horse's reins again.

"Whatever it is, it cannot be good. We must report this immediately to Sangoma."

The horses turned and galloped back down the path toward the dungeons.

Dr. Ichabod turned to Seikh and Philo, whispering, "Sangoma will not like this turn of events."

"Why?" Seikh stood up. "What does the sunlight mean? What does it have to do with Surek?"

"The sunlight means that the prophecy of the chosen one has begun," Philo commented. "And it means Sangoma and his men will not be able to wield as much power."

"Why is that?" Seikh questioned.

"The works of darkness have more difficulty accomplishing anything when the sun shines," Dr. Ichabod explained. "The deeds of Sangoma, Surek, and their men, because they are evil, will be seen for what they are. They will be visible for all to see, and they will be inhibited. Sangoma will certainly have more difficulty performing incantations. And Abaddon . . . well, let's just say his power will not be as potent, which means he will be very angry and will probably cause him to hasten his plans."

"Yes," Philo said. "But the sun will not continue to shine for very long. It will certainly go back in. This is merely the beginning. There's still time."

"You speak truth, Philo," Dr. Ichabod affirmed.

"Well, thank you, Dr. Ichabod! I'm glad you finally recognize that!" Philo commented in an exasperated manner.

"But it's a comfort to know," Dr. Ichabod continued, "that the prophecy is now confirmed by the presence of the light. We can have confidence in our journey."

As they began climbing back up the hill, Philo's words came to pass. The sunbeams disappeared about as quickly as they had appeared. The clouds thickened and the gray skies returned as if they had never seen any light. The three of them trudged wearily up the steep incline, following the fence line that hugged the path that led to the dungeons. Dr. Ichabod limped, holding onto his walking stick with his right hand. Philo led them as usual, with Seikh following behind. Every now and again, Seikh would sneak a look over his shoulder, checking on his father who lingered behind him.

As they reached the top of the incline, Seikh spied a clearing ahead. The trees were thinning, and they would need a plan of escape from Surek's estate. Seikh, Philo, and Dr. Ichabod stopped.

"So, what's the plan from here?" Seikh queried.

"If we are going to expedite this journey, we are going to need some horses," Dr. Ichabod replied, standing with both his hands clasping the top of his walking stick. "Besides, I won't make it otherwise."

"Well," Philo peered through a few bushes while kneeling. "We may be in luck. Come look."

Seikh and his father came closer and knelt on either side of Philo.

"Look there." Philo pointed toward a group of monsters who were gathered on the dirt path that led to the castle's front door.

"Pravitas!" Seikh exclaimed. "And they have some horses. Their dinner no doubt."

Philo nodded.

"Those beasts are ghastly!" Dr. Ichabod moaned, holding his stomach and grimacing.

"You should see them up close," Seikh stated, recalling the torturous night he had spent with them. "And their smell . . ."

"Alright guys," Philo interrupted, "they *have* horses. We *need* horses. I say we *take* their horses."

"And how do you plan to do that?"

"You've got the phanos sword, Seikh," recalled Dr. Ichabod, "and I have a laser whip."

"No," replied Philo immediately, "won't work. Pravitas don't feel much pain, and the whip won't penetrate their thick skin. The sword will, but it's not very long. They could easily use their long arms to attack before Seikh could even reach them. We will have to distract them and then steal their horses. Surely they cannot run faster than we can, including you, Dr. Ichabod."

"That's true," Seikh stated. "They *are* slow."

"Well, then, all we need is a diversion." Philo turned and looked at Seikh.

"Me?"

"Yeah, your father is probably not the best one for the task. And you don't know how to ride very well, do you?"

"I suppose not." Seikh peeked around the bushes that hemmed the three of them in. Three Pravitas stood near the two horses, untying them from a post. Seikh looked at them thoughtfully. "A distraction, huh? Well, alright." Seikh stood straight up and dusted his clothes.

Dr. Ichabod craned his neck and wondered out loud, "And what do you plan to do, Son?"

"You'll see. Just be ready to mount the horses when I draw the Pravitas away."

Without any hesitation, Seikh began walking toward the horses.

"Wait! What are you . . . ?" Philo's voice trailed off as Seikh walked confidently into the clearing where the Pravitas stood.

As Seikh continued toward the Pravitas, he closed his eyes and envisioned the area immediately around him. *I hope my powers work*, he thought as he continued walking slowly. He approached the Pravitas from behind and, picking up a stick, he lightly grazed one of their ears with it.

"Hey!" came a booming voice from the Pravitas he had touched. "Stop that! Not funny!" He smacked the Pravitas next to him.

"Hey! I didn't do nothin', Grammin!" grunted the accused Pravitas, jerking to his left and landing a swift blow on Grammin's upper arm.

"Quit touching me, Olio!" replied Grammin, letting go of the reins to his horse and grappling his attacker by the neck with both hands.

"Stop it, you two!" cried the third Pravitas, casting the reins to his horse to the ground and inserting himself between the two quarreling Pravitas.

"I did not touch you!"

"Then who did?" cried Grammin.

It's working! They can't see me. I'm invisible!

Seikh glanced at the reins dangling from the horses.

And this is going to be easier than I thought.

While the three Pravitas were swatting and hitting each other, grumbling and kicking dust into the air, Seikh swiftly grabbed hold of the reins, yanked the horses around, and started running as fast as he could in the opposite direction. With the horses in tow, Seikh sprinted down the dirt path away from the castle. The Pravitas disappeared in clouds of dust created by the horses' hooves as they hammered the earth.

Just keep running. Keep running! I hope Philo and Father are ready.

Seikh's heart pounded uncontrollably. He could hear the pounding of the Pravitas' large feet as they ran after him, although they could not see him.

"Quick!" yelled Grammin, "Get those horses! Me hungry!"

Seikh looked over his shoulder. The Pravitas were losing ground and their footsteps faded as Seikh ran. He was outrunning them.

Seikh turned around and yelled, "Father! Philo!"

"Right here!" came a voice not too far ahead. Seikh saw his father and Philo standing alongside the dusty path with their arms up, poised to mount the horses.

"Whoa! Whoa! Slow down, Son!" Dr. Ichabod yelled out with a panic-stricken expression on his face.

Seikh dug his feet into the ground and pulled on the reins. "Whoa!" Seikh repeatedly cried out. The horse on his right began slowing down but the one on his left kept racing. As the left horse pulled further ahead, Seikh's arms began to be stretched and he couldn't hold on to both horses any longer. He let go of the reins in his left hand. He continued pulling on the reins in his right hand and was able to bring the horse to a halt.

In one swift motion, Seikh mounted the horse and then held out his hand to his father. "Quick! Get on!"

Dr. Ichabod thrust his right foot into the stirrup, grabbed Seikh's hand, and pulled himself up onto the horse, landing in a sitting position behind Seikh.

"I can't believe I just did that!" his father yelled out.

"Well, you did, so hold on tight!" Seikh yelled as he grabbed ahold of his father's arms and belted them around his waist. "The Pravitas are gaining on us now!"

Seikh dug his heels into the sides of the horse, and it took off like an arrow shot from a bow. The horse's stride was so strong that Seikh and his father slid out of the saddle and onto the backside of the horse. Seikh wrapped the reins tighter around his hands and pulled as hard as he could, lifting his father and himself back into the saddle. Once settled again, Seikh looked sternly forward. Philo had somehow been able to mount the other horse and he was in the lead. Seikh looked behind them. There was no sign of the Pravitas. They had escaped and begun their journey to the Woods of Ivory in search of Lamlorde.

17

The Donkey

The horse ride was brutal. Seikh's backside burned and his legs ached. He did not have much experience riding a horse like his father or Philo. Philo seemed relaxed and confident as the horse glided along the floor of the cluttered forest. His father appeared to take the horse's gallop just as well, despite his disabled hip.

They had outrun the Pravitas rather quickly and pulled off the main path and into the woods. The thickness of the forest demanded that they slow down to a swift trot. They also had to dodge the trees, and this added insult to injury for Seikh. If his aching backside and legs weren't enough, the horse's careening about made him nauseous. His father, although riding well, also didn't seem to appreciate the back-and-forth very much. Seikh had noticed him clearing his throat and slightly moaning every so often since they entered the woods. He then would feel his father's head recline on his back and then lift again.

Hours passed, giving much time for Seikh to think about his mother. How could she have deceived him by masking herself as Pseudomai? How could she have lied to him, leading him into a trap for Surek? It was too much to take in—his own mother had betrayed him. What kind of mother would do this? What had motivated her to turn on him—*and* Father?

Although Seikh knew he had also once been a pawn of Surek's, and ultimately under the control of Abaddon, there was something that turned him. The power of Abaddon had been unleashed but was overcome by the light of The Speech. Why had it penetrated him and changed him but not his mother? Seikh had so many questions. Perhaps when they reached Lamlorde, he could get some answers.

Lamlorde.

The name resounded in his head. It was a strange name, even a mysterious one. Once it had been a name of derision to Seikh. It was mocked and ridiculed as a leftover from mythological stories told by the Dreamers. But now Lamlorde didn't seem mythological at all. Rather, the world of Kosmon seemed mythological—even disordered and out of control. "Death" was a word more appropriate for Kosmon than "life." No hope. No light. No cure for the deadly plague that ailed it. No matter how hard the Scientians might look for a cure, they would never succeed. Death would always reign in Kosmon as long as it perpetuated the lies that Lamlorde was a myth. The cure lay with Lamlorde, and Seikh now knew this. He was convinced of it. All they needed to do was find him to bring healing to Kosmon. The stories of Lamlorde weren't the problem, as Surek thought; Lamlorde was an actual person who held the antidote.

"Whoa!" Seikh heard Philo yell out to his horse.

Coming alongside Philo, Seikh pulled on the reins to his horse, coming to a stop. "What's wrong?" Seikh asked, feeling tired.

"Nothing, really, except being exhausted." Philo stretched his arms out and twisted, popping his back. He then dismounted with a slight thud. "Before we go any farther, it might be instructive for us to take a look at the book, so we know where we need to go next."

"Good idea!" Seikh replied, dismounting.

Standing on the ground, Seikh felt the blood begin to rush back into his legs. He massaged them and stood upright. It felt good to be standing again. He reached up toward his father, grabbed hold of his hand, and helped him down. Philo took the reins of the horses and led them to a nearby tree, tying them up. The forest was getting dark, cool, and misty.

Seikh unloaded the knapsack his father had found at Surek's castle. Holding it out, Seikh declared, "Who wants to do the honors?"

"I think you should, Seikh," Philo answered. "You're the chosen one, after all."

"I agree, Son." Dr. Ichabod echoed.

Seikh slowly untied it. A shimmering white light jumped out and lit up their surroundings. Seikh startled, dropped the knapsack, and covered his eyes.

"What!?" Dr. Ichabod bellowed, using his outer brown robe to cover his eyes. He fell to the ground along with Philo.

"It's the book!" Seikh cried out.

Softly and lowly, a voice spoke, "Take up and read."

Seikh trembled on the ground, frightened but entranced with wonder. Unlike the first encounter he had with the book, Seikh discerned that it was the book talking to him.

A talking book!

Seikh was bewildered. What did this mean? A magical book that shone *and* talked! The book must indeed be magical, and more important than he knew.

"Get up, Seikh! Take the book and read! It's talking to you!" Philo's voice bounced off the trees around them.

Blinded and still on the ground with his eyes closed, Seikh felt around for the book. Grabbing a hold of its smooth, glassy cover, he held the book reverently in front of him and began to open his eyes slowly. Peering through the slits in his eyes, Seikh held the book as it flung itself open and its pages whipped about. The book stopped about midway through.

The voice spoke again. "Read."

Seikh opened his eyes the rest of the way and gazed at the pages. The light that shone from the book was brighter than anything he had ever seen. A warmth radiated from the book. Seikh fixed his eyes on the text which flickered with gold glittering letters. It read:

> *Hear the words of the humble*
> > *And the speech of the lowly spirit;*
> *Ignore the patter of the proud*
> > *And do nothing when you hear it.*

Seikh whispered the words as he read them. When he had finished, the book closed, and the light went out like a candle in the wind. He stood, holding the glassy tome, blinded by the light it had emitted. The forest around him was pitch black, and it was quiet as death.

"What did it say?" Philo whispered.

Seikh turned toward Philo's voice, barely making out his silhouette. "It said that I am to listen to the words of the humble and lowly spirit and ignore those who are prideful." He paused. "What does it mean? And how does this help us find Lamlorde?"

Dr. Ichabod cleared his throat. "It's difficult to say. But we must certainly hold onto the message and not forget it. It will help us find Lamlorde in some way."

Still pondering the words of the book, Seikh stood and returned it to the knapsack and flung it over the horse.

Philo motioned to him and Dr. Ichabod. "Come. Sit down." He patted a large log on the ground. "We must rest before we continue. We can't stop for the night. We gotta keep moving. But let's get a little rest."

Philo handed Seikh and his father something dark and stiff. "Here. Take some and eat. It will help give you some energy."

Sighing with exhaustion, Seikh plopped onto the log next to Philo, taking the food offered to him. It was too dark to see what Philo gave them. He took a whiff of it and placed it slowly on his tongue. It tasted like meat, and it was rather tough and chewy. A sweetness filled his mouth which satisfied his hunger.

"Where did you get this?" Seikh inquired.

"You probably don't want to know." Philo tore off a bite from his portion and chewed with his mouth open.

"You didn't get it from the Pravitas, did you?" Dr. Ichabod asked.

"Like I said, you probably don't want to know."

"Ugh! You took this from the Pravitas?" Seikh's stomach turned, and he began spitting out pieces of food. "What in the world were you thinking? Do you have any idea what they eat?"

"Of course, I do. What do you take me for?" Philo retorted forcefully. "But, hey, it doesn't taste so bad, and you're hungry, aren't you? You don't have any better idea where to get some food, do you?"

"I'd rather die than eat Pravitas food!" Seikh exclaimed, standing up and walking toward his horse.

"Your father doesn't seem to mind."

Seikh turned, "Father, how can you eat that? It's disgusting!"

"It's better than what Surek fed me in his dungeons," Dr. Ichabod gulped. "You'd better eat some, Son. You're going to need the energy."

Seikh stood in front of Philo and his father, watching them devour the food. He began feeling nauseous. As he began to turn back toward his horse, a flicker of light caught his attention.

"What's that?"

"What's what?" Philo replied.

"There's a light a few hundred yards from here. It looks like a camp-fire." Seikh gazed into the distance, studying the light.

Philo and Dr. Ichabod stood and turned.

"Hmm," Dr. Ichabod mumbled, squinting his eyes. "That's a campfire for certain."

"Who would be out here in these thick woods?" Seikh asked.

"It can't be Surek's men or the Pravitas," Philo spoke confidently. "They couldn't have gotten ahead of us."

"I agree," Dr. Ichabod stated. "But we should check it out."

Philo shifted his weight from one foot to the other. "You two should go. I will stay here to keep watch over the horses. If something happens, I will take the horses and catch up with you later at the river's edge."

"That's a good idea," replied Seikh, beginning to take off. "Come, Father."

"Wait a minute!" Dr. Ichabod took hold of Seikh's arm. "Slow down, Son. We will need to take this slowly, so we won't be detected."

"No problem, Father!" Seikh replied, beginning to walk backwards toward the distant campfire. "Remember: I can make myself invisible. I'm in the Infinite. They'll never see me."

With a grunt and a thump, Seikh tripped over some vines and fell to the ground. "I'm alright," he called out, standing and brushing himself off.

Dr. Ichabod, shaking his head, looked at Philo. "I have the feeling that this newfound power of his is going to get him into trouble."

Philo nodded. "Just remember that you have a laser whip, and he has a phanos sword. If all else fails, use them."

With little noise, Seikh and his father made it to the outskirts of the camp-fire. Kneeling behind some brush, Seikh peered into the clearing where the fire glowed orange, lighting the trees around it. No one was around. The only living thing present was a donkey standing on the far side of the fire. The fire cast shadows on its surroundings and smoked floated slowly into the sky.

"I don't see anyone," whispered Seikh. "Do you?"

"No, only a donkey." Dr. Ichabod squatted down. "Make yourself in-visible and go get that donkey. We could use it. I'll stay here." He sluggishly fell to the ground and sat.

Seikh stood up. He scoured the area one more time, and then closed his eyes and envisioned his surroundings. He felt himself disappear among the trees, and he began walking toward the campfire. Becoming invisible was an odd thing. His eyes were closed but he could see everything around him. It felt like he was levitating just inches above the ground, but he was walking normally.

He began searching the outskirts of the camp but found no one. It looked like not one soul had ever been there. There were no footprints and no evidence of a camp being set up. Coming around to the other side of the fire, Seikh found the donkey facing the trees with its backside toward the fire. It was grazing quietly on some tall grass. It seemed to have no aware-ness of his presence.

Approaching the donkey more closely, Seikh observed that it was only about three feet tall. It looked as if it were a foal. Its hair was grey, and it hung its head rather low, even for grazing. It had no saddle or bridle.

Hmm. It must be wild.

"What must be wild?" came a humble, faint voice from the dark.

Seikh looked around but saw no one. Was the donkey talking to him?

The donkey paused chewing some grass, turned toward Seikh, and peered at him with large dark eyes. With his heart racing, Seikh looked behind him and then back at the donkey.

"Are you talking to me?" Seikh asked the donkey.

The low, humble voice spoke again, but this time Seikh could see the donkey's mouth move. "Who else would I be talking to?"

"You can see me? And you can talk?" Seikh stood motionless.

"Of course, I can see you," replied the donkey matter-of-factly. "You are standing there right beside me. And why shouldn't I be able to talk?"

Dumbfounded, Seikh answered, "Why, you are just a brute, dumb beast. How can you talk?"

"Yes," the donkey replied slowly, "that's what some call me: 'brute,' 'dumb beast.' Others call me 'beast of burden.' Still others call me 'humili-ated.' But I still speak."

"How is it that you can see me? I'm in the Infinite and have made myself invisible."

"Hmm," the donkey moaned, turning his head back to his grass. "The Infinite, the Finite. Neither matter to me. They are both present to me, not much of a difference."

"Well, in that case . . ." Seikh opened his eyes and became visible. "There's no reason for me to continue being invisible in the Finite."

The donkey continued chewing on some grass and just stood there quietly. He didn't seem interested in conversation.

"Where did you come from and how did you get here?" Seikh inquired.

Stopping his loud chewing, the donkey repeated the question, "Where did I come from and how did I get here?" He chewed a little more and then turned slowly toward Seikh again. "Hmm," he sighed. "I do not come from anywhere, and I walked here."

"You don't come from anywhere?" Seikh asked, confused.

"Nope," the donkey answered slowly, still eating.

"Is anyone else around here?"

"Nope," he repeated, munching.

"Then who started the fire?"

"Me."

"You?"

"Of course. Who else?"

Seikh looked at the fire and then back at the donkey. "*You* started that fire? How did you do that?"

The donkey stopped eating, looking seriously at Seikh. "With the breath of my mouth." He went back to eating.

Seikh laughed out loud. "Right!"

The donkey turned around, looking in the direction of the campfire once again. "And who is that?"

Seikh turned and saw his father. He had come out from behind the bushes and into the firelight. He stood there looking inquisitive. "Oh, that's my father, Dr. Ichabod."

Seikh's father came closer and stood just in front of the donkey with his eyes wide open, looking puzzled. "Are you talking to this donkey, Son?"

"Well," Seikh spoke awkwardly, "he talked to me first, and so, yeah. I talked back to him."

"A talking donkey?" Dr. Ichabod asked in amazement. "I suppose I've seen and heard stranger things in this world."

"What's strange about a talking donkey?" the donkey asked.

"Oh my," Dr. Ichabod shuddered. "Where did it come from?" he asked Seikh, ignoring the donkey's question.

"From nowhere, he says."

The donkey turned and began grazing again, seemingly disinterested in either of them.

"Wouldn't you like to know where we came from and where we are going?" Seikh asked the donkey.

The donkey sighed, "Hmm."

Seikh and his father looked at each other in bewilderment.

The donkey swallowed his food, turned, and looked at them both. "I know where you are from."

"You do? How?" Dr. Ichabod inquired.

"I know things," the donkey replied plainly.

"Like what?" Seikh asked in disbelief, as if tempting the donkey to provide him solid proof.

"You just came from the Sultan's castle on Black Mountain," he said straightforwardly, "and you are on a journey to find Lamlorde so he can help you find the cure to the plague of Kosmon."

Seikh stood in shock, his eyes widening and his jaw dropping. "How do you know all of this?"

"Like I said," rejoined the donkey, "I know things."

"Well, I suppose you wouldn't mind coming with us on this journey of ours, would you?" Dr. Ichabod looked hopeful. "We could use someone like you to help us travel. I've got this bad hip. It causes me to limp, and it gets mighty painful. Besides, you seem like you would be good company."

"That's why I'm here," the donkey snorted. "To go with you." He paused. "Or you with me."

Seikh and his father looked at each other with wonder. Exactly who was this donkey?

"Seikh," his father spoke confidently, "go get Philo and we can be on our way."

"Hmm," the donkey grunted. "You can't do that." He continued chewing some grass.

"And why not?" Seikh asked indignantly.

"Because he is no longer with you."

"What do you mean he's no longer with us?" Seikh countered, looking around toward the woods where they had left Philo.

"Philo sent you and your father to check out this campfire for a reason," the donkey replied, "so he could return to Surek."

"What? Return to Surek? How can that be? You dumb brute!?" Seikh couldn't believe his ears. Was this donkey deceiving them, too, like everyone else?

"Be careful what you say, dear Seikh." The donkey hung its head, his mouth now emptied of food. "It's wise to listen to the words of the humble rather than the proud."

Seikh recalled the words of the book: *listen to the words of the humble and not the proud*. Was this donkey what the book meant? Was he the humble and Philo the proud?

The donkey tilted its head. "Perhaps it would be helpful if I told you Philo's other name?"

Dr. Ichabod approached the donkey. He cradled the donkey's mouth in his hand and lifted his head. Looking into its eyes, he spoke to it gently. "What other name? What are you talking about?"

Lowly, in a sad, somber voice, the donkey replied, "The Informer."

18

The City of Light

Seikh's thoughts rushed. It had been a trap set for his father and him all along! Philo was the Informer, not his mother! His memory flashed instantly back to the words of Sangoma: *The Informer is still out there somewhere.*

Philo had been the one sent by Surek and for whom Sangoma had been waiting for in the cave. Philo must have decided to wait for him and Pseudomai at his old log house. Pseudomai must have conspired with Philo. They had been working together! Seikh felt naïve—no, stupid. He had listened to the cunning, deceitful words of the proud Philo just as he had listened to Pseudomai—his turncoat mother. His foolishness infuriated him.

Whom could he trust? Surely his father, too, was not a part of the conspiracy? No. He couldn't be. He had been locked up in the dungeon just as he had been. His father's words had too much truth to them to be deceptive, and they rang with authenticity. He seemed humble, and the book directed him to listen to the humble not the proud.

But what—or who—was this donkey? It seemed to know everything about his father and him, and it was very humble. Its words were like sweet morsels. It was a beast which seemed genuine yet mysterious; kind and gentle, yet assertive and confident. An animal who was lost but wanted to be found. There was a quiet strength about it that drew Seikh in.

Bending down on one knee, Seikh looked into the donkey's deep, dark brown eyes. With long, drawn out words, he asked, "Who are you?"

The donkey returned Seikh's stare. His eyes looked sad, but there was a joy behind them. With immediate shock, Seikh knew.

A humble beast of burden.

Seikh stood. His knees began to knock. He spoke with a broken voice, eyes wide open. "You . . . You are Lamlorde!"

The donkey lifted its drooping head and spoke softly. "I am. Do you believe it?"

Seikh's knees weakened, and he dropped to the ground, kneeling in front of the donkey. "Why, yes! Yes, of course!" The words dripped from his lips with relief. He knew that this donkey was indeed Lamlorde.

"I do believe!" Seikh exclaimed.

Behind Seikh, Dr. Ichabod dropped to the ground almost prostrating. "I, too, believe!" he echoed.

"Your journey," began Lamlorde slowly and with intentionality given to every word, "has been difficult. But your journey is not over yet. It's only just begun. You have much still to accomplish. Now that the prophecy about you finding me has been fulfilled, you must take the next step in fulfilling prophecy. But there are preparations that need to be made first."

Lamlorde turned and began walking into the dark forest. Glancing over his right shoulder as he ambled along, he called out, "Come! Follow me!"

Seikh ran after him, leaving his father's side. "Wait!" he dug his heels into the ground, skidding to a stop. "What about the plague? Can you stop it? Can you heal Kosmon? I've found you, and aren't you supposed to have the cure?" Seikh ground his teeth. "Where are you going?"

"Indeed, I have the cure," Lamlorde declared and then paused. "But preparations must be made first. Kosmon is not quite ready for healing. And you must come with me to the Woods of Ivory."

Seikh was troubled in his heart.

Why can't you heal Kosmon now, and stop all this evil?

He grunted in frustration.

"Trust me." Lamlorde spoke firmly, yet pastorally. "I will heal Kosmon. I know you have many questions, Seikh. They will all be answered. But now is not the time. Get on my back."

Seikh looked at his father who was now standing beside him.

"Well, do as he says, Seikh! Don't be foolish and obstinate!" Father exclaimed in a rather gruff voice.

"But what about you, Father?" Seikh responded. "Can't you come with us?"

"His path leads elsewhere," Lamlorde declared. "But do not worry. Your paths will cross again."

Sorrow filled Seikh's heart and tears began to well up in his eyes.

"Father!" Seikh exclaimed, wrapping his arms around him. "Where are you going? How will you be kept safe from Surek?"

"It will be revealed to him where he must go," Lamlorde explained gently. "Do not worry about his safety. The Speech will protect him. Now say your good-byes. We must go."

"Good-bye, Father! I will miss you!" He spoke hesitantly and clung to his father's neck.

"And I you, Son!" he replied lowly. "I am proud of what you have become. You are no longer the rational fool you once were. Now go along with Lamlorde to your destiny and fulfill the prophecy as the chosen one. I will see you again. Remember that I will always love you."

Seikh released his father's neck, quickly wiping the tears from his eyes with his forearm. He turned and mounted the donkey.

"Put your arms around my neck and hold on," Lamlorde commanded. "It's going to be a long yet quick trip."

Seikh bent over, locking his arms around Lamlorde's neck. He peered over his left shoulder toward his father, and with a sniffle he whimpered, "See you later . . . Dad."

Without hesitation, Lamlorde took off with a jerk, causing Seikh to hold onto the donkey's neck for dear life.

The wind rushed over Seikh's body, blowing his hair in every direction as Lamlorde darted through the dark woods. Seikh alternated between grinding his teeth anxiously and biting the inside of his cheek. The scenery around him began to spin like they were in a glass tube. It reminded him of when he ran out of the Hinnom Meadow, escaping the mob which burned the Seers at the stake. Blue light began to appear, streaking all around them. Lamlorde lunged forward even more as they traveled through the familiar space-time tunnel.

How can a donkey run so fast?

He looked down and saw nothing but blurry streaks of light, sparking and turning blue. Lamlorde's feet seemed to race through thin air.

By the time Seikh turned his gaze back over Lamlorde's head, the blue streaking light was spinning like a tornado. Light flashed all around them like lightning. Swirls of racing white clouds appeared. They were enveloped by a blinding white light. He heard voices. One was the voice of his mother. It echoed.

"Seikh, I will always love you. That's what mothers do."

There was a pause, and then his mother cried out in pain.

"Help me, Seikh! I'm so sorry! I deceived you! Please help! I love you!"

Another voice echoed around him.

"Seikh, my best friend!"

It was the sound of Philo, screaming out in pain.

"Philo! Mother!" Seikh called out, but there was no reply.

A cacophony of voices cried out, some in pain and many with apologies.

"Lamlorde! Stop! Don't you hear these voices? We must help them!"

Seikh tugged vociferously at Lamlorde's neck, scraping and scratching his short, stringy mane. But Lamlorde paid no attention. Seikh pulled and clawed at Lamlorde until his strength failed him. His head bent over, hanging alongside Lamlorde's neck. With all his energy expired, he fainted.

"You can open your eyes, Seikh."

Lamlorde spoke with a deep, calming voice. Seikh woke to calm silence. The wind that had raced over them had stopped. Lamlorde was no longer running or moving in the slightest. Curious, yet scared, Seikh opened his eyes slowly. White light shone all about and made it difficult for him to see.

"Your eyes will get used to the light," Lamlorde commented in his humble voice.

Scrambling to find some words, Seikh grunted heavily, "Where are we? I can't see anything. It's so bright!" He covered his eyes with his hands.

"The City of Light," commented Lamlorde.

After a few moments, Seikh's eyes began to adjust to the radiance of his surroundings. The trees were white as snow. The leaves, almond in color, glittered beautifully in a warm yellow sunlight. The ground sparkled as if fresh powdered snow had gently fallen into perfect place. In the distance stood a massive castle on a hill. It was surrounded by numerous immense turrets topped with golden flags waving lazily. The walls of the castle looked whitewashed and glowed as the sunshine struck them. A drawbridge connected the illuminated castle to the mainland over a small moat. Guards in brilliant shining armor lined both sides of the entrance.

Awestruck, Seikh could not help but praise the castle's beauty. "It's so majestic! What is it? Who lives there?"

Lamlorde shook out his mane, which now appeared white and silky, matching the rest of his coat that was now white as snow. "I live here." He turned his head slightly, looking at Seikh who was still on his back. "And those who have been martyred for truth's sake."

Seikh opened his mouth to form another question, and his breath filled the crisp, cool air, making a misty small cloud. But then thoughtfully, he commented, "Those in the Infinite who died because they believed in Lamlorde." His voice trailed off. "You."

"Yes, indeed, Seikh." Lamlorde began to walk leisurely toward the castle. His hooves made imprints in the soft, fluffy substance that looked like snow. No sound was made. Lamlorde's white coat almost blended in with the glistening white ground. It shimmered.

"Why are you white?"

"It would be rather difficult to blend in when in Kosmon if I were shimmering white as I am now, don't you think?"

"So, you disguised yourself?"

"Yes."

"But why?" Seikh asked.

"So that those who have eyes cannot see me, but those who do not have eyes can."

The mysterious riddle made Seikh's heart jump. It added to the gentle yet glorious aura of Lamlorde. He continued to explain. "I had to find you before Surek and his men. You were never going to come to me entirely on your own—too many obstacles—too many things blinding you. That's how it always is with you Kosmonians. I must always seek you first. You never come to me on your own. I must knock, and you must open the door. And Philo, the Informer, was leading you into a trap, although for his own selfish reasons. You were blinded by his pompous confidence—his pride. So, I had to come get you myself and bring you here to the City of Light to prepare for battle. You were never going to make it here on your own."

"Battle?" the word made Seikh bite the inside of his cheek.

"Yes. You are aware of the impending war, are you not? Kosmon has been under siege for thousands of years by the plague. The time has come for it to be destroyed—a final battle to eliminate all the darkness. Sangoma, the ally of Abaddon, has convinced Surek to wipe out the remaining Seers and all the remnants of the Ancient Order—to ring in their 'Telos,' their so-called 'perfect order.' We must come to the Seers' defense; they are helpless in the Woods of Ivory. If we do not help them, darkness will reign forever over Kosmon. We will restore the Ancient Order of things."

He paused, jerked his head around and looked deeply into Seikh's eyes. "And you will help captain the legions organized by The Speech. You have been chosen to meet Surek in this final battle of the war. You will fight for me, and you will lead me to him."

Turning back around, Lamlorde began to ascend the hill that led up to the castle. "You saw Surek's trebuchets he was building behind his castle, yes?"

"Well, yes. But I don't understand," replied Seikh. "Isn't this all about you bringing a cure to Kosmon? To bring an end to suffering and death that the plague has brought? What is this battle? Why should you face Surek?"

"Indeed, Seikh! This *is* about the cure for Kosmon."

Seikh was pensive, sitting like a statue on Lamlorde as they continued up the hill. Without a moment's notice, a thought struck Seikh. "The plague *is* the war, isn't it?"

"In a manner of speaking," replied Lamlorde frankly. "More precisely, it is the effect of the war. The consequences of actions."

"And the plague is not really a disease that infects Kosmonians, is it?" Seikh dismounted Lamlorde with anticipation, laying his hand on his silky white mane. He looked at Lamlorde with apprehension.

"Oh, it is a terrible disease, for sure." His words came out slowly. "It destroys everything. It infects the body, the heart, and the mind of all Kosmonians. It transforms them into something contrary to their designed purposes. But it also infects the trees and the ground—the entire Kosmonian order—making them cursed. No, the plague is not like other diseases. You are correct, Seikh. You are very perceptive. You have learned and matured much through your adventures."

"And the cure . . ." Seikh's eyes widened. As he began forming his words, his mind seemed to take all his thoughts and experiences and piece them together like a puzzle. "And the cure . . . it's not some potion, is it?"

Lamlorde looked at him sorrowfully.

"The cure . . ." Seikh's voiced trailed off. "It's you! *You* are the cure!"

With sad, yet satisfied eyes, Lamlorde spoke. "I am. If you are willing to accept it." Bowing his head low, Lamlorde turned toward the castle. "Lead me to the drawbridge."

As they approached the top of the hill, Seikh observed creatures that looked like lions on each side of the drawbridge. They had a white coat of hair that glistened in the sun, and two wings stretched out above each of them.

As they prepared to cross the drawbridge, the lion creatures bowed their heads low. "Lord! Master!" they called out.

"Follow me," Lamlorde spoke calmly to Seikh. "You can cross only by my power."

Slowly crossing, Seikh followed Lamlorde closely and silently. The lion-like creatures did not make a sound as they bowed in adoration. The sense of honor was palpable, the feeling of awe indescribable. The creatures paying homage to Lamlorde was something Seikh had never encountered.

Such reverence. Such respect. And for a donkey!

Lamlorde glanced back, as if he could read Seikh's thoughts. Seikh felt guilty, and then he felt unworthy to be in Lamlorde's presence.

When they reached the other side of the drawbridge, Lamlorde stopped, and another lion-like creature emerged from their right and bowed.

"Jonathan, my good servant, is the table prepared?" Lamlorde asked in his usual melancholy tone.

"Yes, my Lord. Everything is ready."

"Good. Thank you. Let the supper commence."

Jonathan turned briskly and disappeared around a wall of the castle. A door was heard closing and clanking with a locking sound. Lamlorde turned and began walking toward the castle. Seikh followed. Directly in front of them stood two large doors, standing at least three times taller than Seikh. But there was something peculiar about them. They had no knobs or handles. There was no way for someone to enter from the outside. But Lamlorde continued sauntering toward them as if expecting to enter the castle through them.

Two guards, one on each side of the doors, wearing white shining armor, dropped to one knee. They proclaimed, "You are worthy, Lamlorde!"

Then, slowly, the two doors clicked and began opening inward. They creaked as Lamlorde began to enter the castle. Seikh, following closely behind, stared at the guards in awe.

Once inside, Seikh noticed immediately that they were in a dining hall. Large white pillars lined the center of the hall in two rows, holding up a cathedral ceiling that seemed to stretch to the sky. The floor appeared as a spotted dark marble. In between the two rows of pillars stood a large and exceptionally long table. The opposite end of it could not be seen, and creatures he had never seen before sat at the table. They had smooth skin with different colors, and they wore white robes. A delicious smell wafted through the air. Seikh could not believe his eyes—it was almost exactly what he had seen in his dream!

"You recognize this, do you?" Lamlorde inquired.

"Yes!" Seikh exclaimed, staring around the palace and investigating every object.

"This was similar to your vision, Seikh. Your dream showed you what once was and will yet be." Lamlorde led the wide-eyed Seikh down the right side of the banquet table.

Seikh began to understand. "Why, yes, of course!" he spoke slowly. "This is how Kosmon once was. It was a place of peace, joy, and fulfillment!"

Lamlorde nodded.

"The Ancients loved each other," Seikh continued. "They cared for each other and ate with one another. But then something wicked happened, and it turned the Ancients against each other, like they turned against each other in my dream, eating uncontrollably and hating each other." Seikh's face grew long. "What happened, Lamlorde? What made them hate each other?"

"Like succulent meat on a platter," Lamlorde explained, "Abaddon offered one of the Ancients kingship over Kosmon."

"Sangoma!"

"Yes. Abaddon gave Sangoma powerful magic. This magic was powerful enough to seduce the Ancients into believing they could become gods, molding their own destinies. This is the plague, Seikh: belief in one's self. All the things that characterize Kosmon—the darkness, transmutation, death—are all effects of the plague."

"So, what does Sangoma get out of this?"

"Perpetual kingship over Kosmon. At least, that's what he thinks. Abaddon had no right to give this power to Sangoma in the first place."

"And what did Abaddon get in return?"

"To spit in The Speech's face."

Seikh was confused and scratched his head. Lamlorde explained, "Abaddon got the opportunity to rewrite what The Speech had authored: Kosmon."

19

The Plan

S eikh's eyes skimmed across all the creatures who sat around the banquet table. All had been summoned by Lamlorde to take on Sangoma, and ultimately Abaddon, and he was to lead them into this final battle. He felt a heavy sense of responsibility, but he felt humbled and unable to fulfill his prophecy. Yet Lamlorde seemed to have all confidence in him. He was the chosen one.

Lamlorde continued to lead Seikh down the side of the table when their promenade was interrupted by a familiar voice.

"Seikh, my boy!"

A Seer dressed in white stood up from the table beside them. He let out a loud chuckle.

"Elihu?" Seikh exclaimed in surprise. "What are you doing here?"

"Ahh, come now, son. You should know the answer to that question," Elihu said smiling. "I've been here since the day Surek put that light arrow right through me!"

He chuckled again, but louder, as if he thought it was really humorous and patted Seikh on the back with a thud.

"I see you have come to accept the truth, or else you wouldn't be here, would you?" His chuckle quieted and trailed off. "Well, welcome to reality, son, where the Infinite and Finite meet."

Seikh felt confused and gave off a look of bewilderment.

Lamlorde spoke up, "Not everything has been explained to him yet, General. You will need to excuse his ignorance at this time."

"General?" inquired Seikh, looking befuddled.

"Why, yes! Good Lamlorde here bestowed upon me the honor of General in this final battle for Kosmon. Think of it, Seikh! A Seer like me a General!" He patted Seikh on the back again with a thud, making him almost fall over.

Seikh felt somewhat uncomfortable with Elihu's joviality. He was accustomed to his seriousness. What had happened to change his demeanor? It must have been his welcome to Lamlorde's palace. Everyone there seemed quite cheerful.

"Well, Seikh," continued Elihu, "take a look around. This is where the Infinite and Finite meet. The things of the physical world, Kosmon, is the Finite. The things beyond them are the Infinite, the place where Lamlorde lives, Abaddon, and me!" He slammed Seikh on the back again, causing Seikh a little pain this time and some gritting of his teeth. "Those who have eyes to see can perceive both and live in both. They have come to see reality as it really is."

"But, Lamlorde, didn't you say that everyone who lives here has been martyred for truth's sake? So aren't they all dead?" Seikh looked around at all the different-colored smiling faces.

"Yes," Lamlorde quickly responded. "But not all of them have been martyred. Just the Seers you see before you. The ones who were burned at the stake in the Hinnom Meadow and killed in the City of Petra."

"Others," interrupted Elihu, "like Jinn over there," he pointed to a creature standing just on the other side of the table who was conversing with a Seer in shimmering white, "he is actually still physically living in Kosmon. Outside the Seers, Jinn is just one among the very few living in the Finite of Kosmon who have come to the truth of The Speech and Lamlorde. He was able to see and live in the Finite and Infinite at the same time, just like the Seers." He turned toward Seikh. "That's what I was trying to get you to understand at my house in Petra. See, it can be done! Difficult, but it's possible. All things are possible with The Speech."

The Finite and the Infinite. All one reality.

Seikh began to make sense of it. He thought back to when he awoke from his vision on the dreadful night of the fate of the Seers: he was already dead. He was living in the Infinite, but he thought he was still living in the physical Finite of Kosmon. He had been going in and out of the Finite and Infinite. This is why some of the Kosmonians could see him and sometimes they could not. He must have been in the Finite at the time of the massacre of the Seers. This explained why they were able to hear him and then chase after him. And Philo! He had taught him how to see the Infinite more clearly and how to make himself unseen in the Finite by closing his eyes and concentrating on the Infinite. This meant that Philo had been dead all along, too, or at least knew about the Infinite.

"If someone knows the existence of both and has the eyes to see," Seikh wondered aloud, "then he can live in both the Infinite and the Finite *at the same time.*"

"Yes, my son! You got it." Elihu's voice resounded.

"Then Sangoma knows this! He can use it to his advantage! And there is no hiding from him!"

"He already has," Lamlorde replied. "He has successfully used Abaddon's forces from the Infinite to convince most Kosmonians that only the Finite exists, that the Seers are raving mad, and to promote ideas that intensify the plague and keep it spreading. He has worked his way into Surek's cabinet, making it possible for him to rule perpetually. Surek is just Sangoma's pawn for destroying whatever is left of the Ancient Order, including the Seers. Surek does not know what he is doing. He is not even aware that his nature has changed. He has been blinded by his power."

Lamlorde was looking at the floor. Seikh sensed a deep sadness in his heart. Lamlorde lifted his head and looked directly at Elihu. "It's time to begin, General."

"Yes, sir," Elihu replied, swiftly turning around and walking briskly down the side of the elongated table.

"Come, Seikh," Lamlorde spoke more firmly. "Follow me and take your place at the table."

Seikh followed Lamlorde down the side of the table toward the entrance of the palace. Lamlorde walked more quickly, and he seemed to have more confidence and a sense of resolve. As they approached the head of the table, Seikh noticed a large throne placed where all could see. It was covered with gold and padded with crimson silk. It sat upon a rather large, square pedestal also covered with gold. A chair just as large sat to the right of it. In one swift yet gentle motion, Lamlorde sprang up onto the throne on the right. A deafening silence fell upon the banquet hall. Everyone stood at attention.

"You may be seated," Lamlorde cried out. He then turned to Seikh, "You may take your seat."

Seikh was confused.

Is this throne really mine?

His thoughts rushed. Adrenaline pumped through his veins. He bit his lip and then approached the throne to sit down.

"Not there young one," Lamlorde spoke softly yet firmly. "As valuable and significant as you are, you are not God."

"Oh! I'm so sorry. I didn't . . ." Seikh began trembling and jumped straight up as if at attention.

"Here you are, General." Elihu stood next to him, holding out a solid oak chair. "Your seat."

General?

Shocked, Seikh placed his hand on the rough wooden seat and sat down slowly, inspecting everyone around him.

How am I a General?

He bit the inside of his cheek nervously. All eyes were on Lamlorde, except his.

I don't know what I'm doing. How can I lead anyone?

The battle for confidence still warred inside of Seikh.

Lamlorde sat down on his throne. He began to speak, his voice echoing throughout the hall. "We shall begin our plans for the battle against the dark forces of Abaddon."

In unison, everyone replied, "We shall follow you, Lord!"

"General Elihu will lead his troops to rescue what is left of the Seers who are living in the Finite in the Woods of Ivory. He will bring them to the Plain of Gemar where the final battle will take place. He will lead them from the east."

"Yes, Lord!" cried out all who sat around Lamlorde's table. "It shall be so."

"General Seikh, who also lives in the Infinite and can traverse into the Finite, will gather those who remain in Kosmon who are believers in the reestablishment of the Ancient Order. He will lead them to Gemar from the west."

"Sir Lamlorde," Elihu spoke up, "who shall be leading those in the Infinite who follow you and have taken their seat next to you in your palace at the table?"

"I will," replied Lamlorde in a deep voice. "We shall gather on the south side of Gemar. General Elihu and General Seikh, we must all be at Gemar in three days."

Seikh's thoughts raced.

How can I lead those who still believe in the Ancient Order? How will I know who they are? Where will I find them in only three days?

The lack of self-assurance continued to plague him.

Lamlorde turned to Seikh and replied softly as if he had read his mind. "Do not worry, Seikh. You and Elihu shall have everything you need to fulfill your duties. Only be strong and courageous. Do not fear. Continue to kill your ego. Trust in me."

Lamlorde stood to dismiss everyone. The crowd stood with him. In unison, it lifted the chalices that had been placed neatly in front of each of them on the table. "All hail the King!" they cheered.

After taking a drink, they placed the chalices upon the table and began to disperse. In straight lines led by commanding officers, they filed down the different hallways leading out of the banquet hall. Some went down the two hallways on the left and others down the two hallways on the right.

Seikh stood up from his hard chair, not knowing which way to go, when a person of immense stature approached him. He stood about nine feet tall and wore a white robe just like the Seers and looked much like Seikh with long white hair interspersed with brown.

"Archippus," Lamlorde commanded, "take General Seikh to the weapons quarter and prepare to send him off on his mission."

"Yes, my Lord," Archippus replied in a deep, resounding voice.

Following Archippus down one of the long, straight hallways made Seikh feel very small and undignified. Archippus's physique was overly intimidating, and he could not see around him to where they were going. After marching several hundred yards, Archippus turned abruptly to the right, entering through a white door as it opened on its own. Entering the room, the door closed gently behind them and latched. The room had four radiant white walls and a floor that shone like the sun had outside the castle. The room was sterile and empty.

Archippus swiveled and spoke lowly. "Seikh."

"Yes, sir?" Seikh answered nervously.

"There's no need to address me as 'sir.' I am your servant."

Seikh was still trying to get accustomed to being in a place of respect and being called a General. It made him feel uneasy.

"Archippus," Seikh addressed the large figure in front of him while looking about the room, "there are no weapons here. There is *nothing* in here."

"Yes, you are correct, General. Lamlorde secretly instructed me to bring you to this room for privacy, so I could give you specific instructions for your mission."

"But what about my weapons?" Seikh asked curiously.

"Your weapons are not here. You actually have a two-part mission. In addition to gathering those who believe in the reestablishment of the Ancient Order, you are to retrieve the Book of Zoe and the phanos sword from Philo. Those are your weapons. Your retrieval of them is imperative. The success of the battle depends upon it."

"But how will I get them?" Seikh asked. "I don't know where to find Philo. Besides, he is stronger than I am and can wield the sword. I cannot do any such thing. I don't even know how to fight."

"You do not need to know how to fight, General Seikh. The Speech will lead you to Philo, and you will take the book and sword with ease. Just trust in Lamlorde and his power."

Alarmed and dismayed, Seikh blurted out, "But this is going into a battle blind!"

"Calm, my General." Archippus placed his large hand upon Seikh's frail shoulder. "Sometimes, blind trust is all you have. But trust can be an anchor. The Speech will not let you fail."

Seikh took a deep breath. The brilliance of the room was beginning to overwhelm his eyes. Perhaps that is why tears began to well up in them.

Breathe and trust. I can do this. No. I cannot do this, but The Speech can through me.

A single tear began to run down his cheek. Archippus wiped it.

Yes, now you understand, spoke a voice inside Seikh's mind. He recognized the soft soothing voice. It was The Speech. *Listen to Archippus!*

"It is time, General. You must go." With swift movement, Archippus left the room through the shimmering white door, and Seikh followed.

Flowing graciously down the corridor, Archippus led Seikh through multiple, winding hallways and large white doors until they came to a spherical foyer. Two doors with arches at the top stood directly in front of them. Archippus stopped, placed his arm around Seikh's shoulders. The side embrace was warm. It felt as if a sense of joy and peace began to pour into him. Seikh had never felt anything like it before. The most similar sensation was when he first met Elihu, and he began to believe in Lamlorde. That feeling, though, had been temporary, fleeting. This sensation filled his soul, and it remained upon him for some time.

Archippus, ushering Seikh, proceeded slowly toward the doors. They opened. Light streamed into the foyer. Seikh took a heavy breath and exhaled. It was time. The hour for which he had been chosen had come. Although nervous, he felt something like a hand strike his cheek warmly and his nerves began to relax. He began to feel confident, something he had never felt much before. Vigor and strength began to swell slowly within him. He knew that The Speech in the power of Lamlorde was with him.

Seikh and Archippus walked through the exit and into the warm sunlight. Archippus's arm dropped from Seikh's shoulders. Seikh turned and gave a nod to the towering figure. In his warm, low voice, Archippus bid Seikh farewell, blessing him with "it shall be so." Seikh echoed the blessing. He turned. Down the hill he marched away from the City of Light. Trudging over the bridge to the other side of the castle's moat, Seikh once again was sucked up by the space-time tunnel.

20

Armageddon

Seikh found himself deposited in the Hinnom Meadow. He was beginning to get used to traveling by The Speech's power in the space-time tunnel, but it still left him disoriented coming out of it. Somewhat nauseated, he stood up and quickly noticed that he was alone. Kosmon was dark and overcast as usual. It was, however, eerily quiet.

Seikh scanned the meadow thoughtfully.

Where is everyone?

His eyes roved back and forth, searching for any kind of life. He caught a glimpse of blackened grass and charred trees. It was where the Seers had been martyred. He walked to the place his father had spoken on that dreadful night. The grass crunched and dissipated into black dust underneath his feet as he walked. Bending down on one knee and touching the ground with his hand, Seikh felt a sense of sadness.

"Sad, isn't it?" a voice abruptly said behind him.

Seikh rose and turned. About twenty feet away stood the most grotesque creature he had ever laid eyes on. It had long black and brown mangled hair and black eyes. Its nose was barely distinguishable from the rest of its face, and it was wearing a gray, tattered robe stained with what looked like blood. On its back was a pack made of something scaly with a long tail drooping to the ground.

"But it doesn't have to be like this," the creature continued. Its voice seemed familiar to Seikh. Its head bowed slowly as it began to walk in a zigzag fashion toward him. It lifted its eyes, looking deeply into Seikh's. "We can finally make Kosmon what it was meant to be. Did you hear? We have the cure now. We just have to complete the extinction of those who refuse to accept the cure and want to hold on to fairytales." It looked thoughtfully into Seikh's eyes as if reading his mind and then continued, "True, it's very sad that it has to be done. But they are just so stubborn. Progress can be made only if they are eliminated. Surek has his army ready. He wants you to help lead it. Just believe in yourself, Seikh."

Perplexed, Seikh gazed at the creature as his heart began to palpitate. "Your voice. It seems . . . Who are you?"

"Surely, you know who I am," the creature retorted with amazement. "We've been friends for so long!"

"Philo?"

"Why, yes. Don't you know your best friend when you see him?"

"But you have changed! I don't recognize you at all. You," Seikh fumbled for the words to say. "You . . ." He didn't want to say the word that came to his mind.

"I'm what?"

"Hideous," Seikh responded sheepishly. "You aren't yourself."

"Why, of course I'm myself! I've only grown to be more of what I wanted to be all along. I am beautiful!" He held up his arms. The tattered robe hung from his limbs like scraps of grave clothes. "Look at me! I've never been better. I'm the best version of myself. Why, I am like a rose! I'm almost like a god."

Seikh peered at him in disgust and disbelief. "Do you really not see what you have become? You are under the control of Surek and Abaddon, and this has led you to evolving into something hideous. Put away your pride! Let go of your ego! Turn to Lamlorde to be cured!"

Philo growled harshly and slurred his words, "No! No!" He grabbed the sides of his head with his disfigured hands. "This can't be! You! It is *you* who has changed. You don't see what *you* have really become!" His eyes grew wide and intense, piercing Seikh's soul. "I have become my true self! I have followed my heart! This is the path to wholeness. I control my life! I'm in charge!"

"No, Philo, or should I say 'Informer?' You have only puffed yourself up with pride, thinking yourself a god!" Philo began to circle around him slowly, but Seikh continued. "Listen to me, Philo! I'm your best friend. I know and have found the cure. Kill your ego and come with me! It's the only way to be set free."

"No!" Philo grumbled lowly. "You have become irrational just like the Seers, believing in fantasies and myths! And to think that I was somewhat hesitant to help Surek find you, my so-called best friend. I even taught you how to travel between the Finite and Infinite! I trusted you with knowledge from the Greater Power. Surek was right. You are a traitor! You should have joined the Scientians and Transmutants when you had a chance. We are the ones who have the cure. We are becoming gods! And it's people like you who need to be eliminated. The time has come for your kind to come to an end!"

Reaching inside the scaly pack, Philo drew out the phanos sword.

"Don't do this, Philo! We are friends!" Seikh screamed in desperation. "It will not end well for you!"

"No. It won't end well for *you*. If you will not join Surek, you must die!"

Philo charged Seikh. His hideous frame was weak, and he wobbled as he ran toward him, making it easy for Seikh to dodge the oncoming attack. As Philo thrust the sword, Seikh sidestepped and tripped him. Falling to the ground, Philo's arms hammered the solid ash, knocking loose the phanos sword into the air. It landed several feet away. In one swift action, Seikh darted for the sword. In the process, he stepped on Philo's back, smashing his face into the ground. Diving, Seikh stretched out his hand to grasp the fallen sword. Philo jumped onto his back and began pummeling him. Seikh rolled over repeatedly, wrestling Philo and pinning him to the ground. With the phanos sword now in Seikh's hand, the yellow and red blade lit with a loud hum. Philo turned swiftly, wriggling his arm loose and began strangling Seikh. The sword dropped to the ground. Philo's deformed fingers dug deeply into Seikh's throat, nails piercing his skin.

Straining to speak, Seikh forced out the only words he could utter. "Stop! I don't want to hurt you!"

With a rapid motion, Seikh struck Philo's arm with his right fist, breaking it in half like a dead branch. Philo's other arm then struck Seikh on his cheek, causing blood to spurt out as he thrust him flat into the ground. Seikh raked his hands all around, trying to find anything to hit Philo. Grasping what he thought was a rock with his right hand, Seikh thrust his arm up quickly to strike Philo. In a split second, Philo recognized in horror that he had seized the phanos sword. It lit, and the red and yellow blade pierced Philo's head. He fell to the ground, dead.

Seikh screamed. "No!"

Philo glowed red and began to dissipate. He then disappeared with a gale force wind. All became quiet.

Seikh's heart was thumping and skipping, and he was out of breath.

No! What have I done? My best friend! I could have helped him. I could have turned him to Lamlorde's side!

He dropped the sword, and the handle clanged as it hit the ground. He sobbed with his face in his hands as he kneeled upon the ash.

There's nothing you could have done, Seikh, said a voice inside his head. This time he recognized the utterance. It was The Speech. *He was utterly lost, and no other circumstance would have made it different. Now rise and go forward.*

After several minutes passed, he slowly began to regain his composure. He rose from the ground. Through tear-soaked eyes, he caught a glimpse of Philo's pack. It laid in the dark ash on the ground, and it was glowing. Reaching slowly for it, he opened it. A bright light shot out of the pack and blinded Seikh.

The Book of Zoe!

Holding one hand over his eyes, he reached in and pulled it out. The bright light faded. On the front was the word *Zoe*. Handling it gently, he opened it. In a flash, just as before, its pages turned vigorously and then stopped abruptly at a passage. It read:

> *Blessed are the righteous;*
> 　　*They listen to wisdom,*
> *Taking instruction of Lamlorde,*
> 　　*And following him to victory!*
> *Flame, fire, destruction!*
> 　　*The ways of those who*
> *Say there is no knowledge and*
> 　　*All is perception.*
> *But the wise accept knowledge;*
> 　　*They seek truth, and in truth*
> *They find life and escape*
> 　　*The penalty of depravity.*
> *The chosen one goes before Me*
> 　　*In the breath of The Speech,*
> *Warning those of what is to come,*
> 　　*Lamlorde's justice entirely.*
> *He goes north and then to the East,*
> 　　*Asking, "Are you with Lamlorde?"*
> *Every person and every beast;*

To the Plain of Gemar he rests.

Seikh absorbed the words like a sponge soaking up water. He could not believe his eyes.

The prophecy! This is about me!

He then recalled Lamlorde's words to him before his departure from the City of Light: *Do not worry . . . You shall have everything you need to fulfill your duties. Only be strong and courageous. Do not fear.*

He now had everything he needed—the sword and the Book of Zoe, which instructed him what he needed to do. Slowly closing the book, he reached for the pack, as gruesome as it was. He placed the book and sword into it, latched it, flung it over his shoulder, and began northward into the Woods of Ebony. Behind him, nestled in the woods just to the south several hundreds of yards away, was the old log cabin he once lived in. He did not think of it, and he never desired to see it again.

As night began to fall and a heavy darkness settled upon all of Kosmon, Seikh's legs were tight and sore, and the bottom of his feet ached. He had been traveling all afternoon and evening without stopping, neither eating nor drinking anything. He was weak and tired, but the trek was uneventful, and he saw no one. It continued to be eerily silent throughout the woods. Pausing at a tree that had fallen over the path he was taking, he laid the sack upon the ground and took a seat.

The stillness around him felt intimidating and daunting, but he knew that the power of Lamlorde was with him. At this thought, a sense of peace began to fill him. It was like a gentle breeze that tickles the branches of a tree, or how warm honey slowly seeps down one's parched throat. It was therapeutic, as if there were not a problem in all of Kosmon. He was unfamiliar with such an intense sensation. He refrained from biting the inside of his cheek. He closed his eyes. Unexpectedly, the dead, crunchy leaves on the blackened trees began to rustle softly. He opened his eyes and could see very little. Just a few beams of moonlight shone through the treetops, casting a few shadows along the ground.

The throbbing in his legs and feet began to subside, so he stood, preparing to continue his journey north. As he flung the sack over his shoulder, he heard feet walking and crunching through the leaves. The steps were slow and steady, and then they stopped. He could see no one. Remembering the words of the prophecy in the book, he called out, "Are you with Lamlorde?"

It was quiet, and then a low voice answered, "Who is asking?"

"I am," Seikh replied confidently and courageously, retrieving the phanos sword and lighting its bright yellow and red blade. "General Seikh of the army of Lamlorde."

"Seikh?" the voice responded.

Seikh turned to the left. He aimed the sword toward the voice, lighting a figure only yards away. "Father?"

"Seikh! Yes! Yes, I am with Lamlorde!" said his father as he wobbled toward him. "My son!"

Embracing each other, his father began to weep. "It felt like I would never see you again!"

"Why, I have only been gone a very short time!"

"What are you talking about? It's been months since Lamlorde took you away to the Woods of Ivory!"

"Then time must be different here because I was gone only for part of a day when I was with Lamlorde."

"Oh, Seikh, my boy! It's been months here, and much has changed since you have been gone. Surek now has an entire army and a full arsenal. They are headed to the Plain of Gemar."

"Where is everyone else? The Seers?" Seikh inquired.

"What was left of the Seers hid in the Woods of Ivory, as you know. But even the few remaining in Kosmon who had not initially fled are now hiding there. Not a one is left here in Kosmon. The Transmutants and Scientians have all moved near Black Mountain. They are all under Surek's power."

"Surely not all of them are under his power," replied Seikh. "Lamlorde has given me the task to gather whoever has not bowed the knee to Surek and lead them to the west side of the Plain of Gemar."

"Well," Seikh's father retorted, "there is a small group of Kosmonians hiding not too far from here. They make their living underground, keeping to themselves for as long as I can remember. I don't know much about them. It's a small group, maybe twenty or thirty. But why would Lamlorde want you to take them to Gemar? Surek's army will be there. Surely, they will slaughter you."

"Perhaps," Seikh spoke hesitantly. "But we will be protected by the power of Lamlorde."

"Lamlorde? The donkey? How will a donkey protect you? What we need is The Speech."

"He is much more than a donkey, Father. He is much more powerful than the eye beholds. Lamlorde and The Speech, well, one cannot have one without the other. It's like they're almost the same."

"The same?" Seikh's father seemed perplexed. "If that's the case, then perhaps we can trust a donkey with our lives. But I must say, it is a mystery."

"Yes, I'm coming to the conclusion that there are a great many mysteries about this world. Not everything can be understood by mere reason."

Seikh's father examined him with his soft eyes. "You are becoming wise, Son. Wise indeed."

Seikh placed his hand upon his father's shoulder. "You must come with me, Father. Lamlorde's orders. Everyone who is on his side must come with me to the Plain of Gemar."

"I can't," he retorted. "I'm not able. My hip is worse, and my limp is a grave disability. I would be no help in this battle."

"Don't speak like that, father! If there is anything I am learning, it is that Lamlorde has a purpose for each of us, including you."

With a smile and a tap on Seikh's shoulder, his father happily agreed. "Then let's go, my boy. Let's finish this."

By morning, Seikh and his father had reached the northern edge of the Woods of Ebony. Stopping for only a couple of hours to rest, they had made good time. The Kosmonians who were living underground were just a short distance to the west. Looking upon the small, oval-shaped hills with large stones scattered among them, Seikh's thoughts dwelled upon his mission—gathering all who were left and preparing for the Ancient Order to be reestablished.

"I believe," Seikh's father began, interrupting Seikh's thoughts, "the group of Kosmonians who live there are led by Anna, the mother of a primitive clan, the Sibyls. She must be quite old by now, if she's even alive. Like I said before, I don't know much about them. No one does. There's no telling how they will take to our encroachment, or if they will even talk to us."

"We have to try," Seikh replied. "We have only one more day to get to Gemar. Tomorrow is the third day. Lamlorde's command. So, it shall be."

Taking a step in the direction of the stones, Seikh's father poked his walking stick into the ground with a grunt. Sighing, he began softly speaking. "You know, I've been meaning to tell you what happened to your mother."

"I know what happened. She's a pawn of Surek now. She's been deceived by Abaddon and his puppet Sangoma." Sadness welled up inside as he spoke.

"That's not what I mean," Seikh's father said. "When you left with Lamlorde, I was led back toward Surek's castle by The Speech. Along the way, I found your mother in the woods. I was following her from a distance, so she didn't know I was there. She was with Philo, I suspect, looking for you and me. After a little time, Philo left her and headed back to the castle, I suppose. This gave me the chance to talk to her alone.

"I was somewhat scared she would take me back to the dungeons, but as I approached her, I could tell she was not doing well. She looked old, and she was coughing. I put my arm around her. She looked at me, but she couldn't say anything. My arm seemed too heavy for her, and she bent over from its weight and fell to the ground. I tried to help her up, but she discouraged me. The plague had gotten her, Son. She was on the edge of death.

"I spoke to her, Seikh, but she couldn't speak to me. She hardly had any breath. She collapsed fully to the ground. Then she reached up, touching my face. I could tell she still loved me. I softly stroked her cheek. She was so frail and wrinkled. Cold. She wasn't herself, Son. Her appearance was horrible. It took everything I had to keep looking at her.

"Her lips began to quiver, but no sound came out. She looked apologetic. And as I was about to tell her how we had found Lamlorde and that she could be cured if I just took her to him, she took her last breath. She died right there in front of me, Seikh. She glowed and disappeared. Forever."

Seikh's father began to weep, and his walk slowed. Seikh wrapped his arm around him. How he wished his mother would have chosen the path of Lamlorde, to have passed through! But it was not meant to be. She had made her choice. She had been blinded by the ideas of the Transmutants. And now she was dead.

"Maybe, Father," Seikh spoke hopefully, "Mother will somehow still make it. The Finite is not the end. We all must enter the Infinite at death. Maybe, just maybe, she made it to Lamlorde after all."

As they approached the small, stone earthen village, Seikh's nerves were on edge.

What will these people say? What will they do?

Seikh knew his duty: he must call out, asking them whether they were for Lamlorde or not.

But where does their allegiance lie? Who are these Kosmonians anyway?

He had never heard of them, and he knew he must be prepared for anything, even if it meant using his phanos sword.

Seikh stepped down onto a narrow descending staircase made of stone. It led to a small wooden door, which by appearance was the front door to a small house built into the ground. With his father right behind him, Seikh rapped on the door quietly. No sound. He waited. No answer. He rapped again, and the door cracked open slowly.

"Who is it?" said a small, feminine voice.

"It's General Seikh of the army of Lamlorde," Seikh replied confidently. "Are you for the reestablishment of the Ancient Order?"

The door slammed shut. Seikh and his father glanced at each other.

A voice surrounded them. "I am Anna, Mother of the Clan of Sibyl." A pause. "I am committed to Lamlorde and the Ancient One, who is to reestablish the Ancient Order. You are the chosen one, the one foretold long ago who would find Lamlorde, bringing the cure for death. What is it that you require?"

Seikh glanced at his father again. His father nodded.

"Speak!" Anna cried out.

"Lamlorde has sent me to gather all Kosmonians dedicated to the reestablishment of the Ancient Order, and to Lamlorde, who brings the cure. I am to lead any who are willing to come with me to the Plain of Gemar. We are to be there by tomorrow."

The door flung open. Standing there as straight as a board was a Seer, all white.

"So it is time!" the Seer spoke.

"Anna?" Seikh questioned.

"Yes."

"You're a Seer!" Seikh said in surprise.

"Yes, I am, along with my clan." Other Seers, short and tall, began to peer from behind her. "And so are you! You, the chosen one! I never thought I would see this day. My ancestors have spoken the prophecy and waited for this moment for hundreds of years while in hiding, away from those bloodthirsty Scientians and Transmutants. And it has come!"

"Yes!" Seikh exclaimed joyfully. "The time has come for the plague to be destroyed. Lamlorde is coming! We are to prepare for war."

The journey east to Gemar was more arduous than anticipated by Seikh. The terrain was rough. Rocks and ruts littered the ground. Exposed tree roots, jutting from underneath the sod and winding to-and-fro, made it even more difficult to navigate. The only reprieve was that the Woods of Ebony had thinned, allowing more light to expose the tattered landscape so some of the obstacles could be avoided.

Thankfully, the Sibyl Clan had left all their belongings behind, which made the trek less laborious. No food, drink, or weapons to carry—just themselves. Anna had directed them to leave everything. Seikh had the Book of Zoe and the phanos sword and that was enough, she had said. Lamlorde would provide anything else if they needed it.

With Seikh in the lead and the Sybils and Seikh's father following, up and down and around they went, hurdling and stumbling over the land's flora. For hours they had traveled, and darkness had begun to fall—the eve of the final battle was upon them.

Twisting and turning, Seikh was dizzy and nauseated. Anxiety flowed through his veins, and his stomach churned. He was hungry, and he felt dehydrated.

Surely Gemar isn't much further!

He began biting his lip, hoping to distract himself from his discomfort. He suddenly wondered about his father.

"Father!" Seikh called out, turning around.

"Yes, Son?" came a reply.

"How are you holding up? Are you okay?"

Seikh caught a glimpse of a silhouette through the dark that looked like his father's. It was wobbling, and a walking stick moved up and down beside it. "Well," he said gasping for air, "I would have taken a different route!" He chuckled and then coughed.

"We shouldn't be too far from Gemar now," Seikh called back.

He lifted his head and looked up to the treetops toward the horizon. Just to the left, he spied something out of the ordinary, poking up from behind the trees. It almost looked like a row of small baskets off in the distance.

Trebuchets!

Seikh stopped, his heart beating restlessly.

"What is it?" Anna asked, coming to an immediate halt.

"Look there!" Seikh pointed to the treetops. "Trebuchets!"

"And so we are near Gemar now," Anna replied. "That must be Surek's army. It is almost dark. We should camp here for the night and then rise early to meet Lamlorde and the others."

"I think you're right, Anna." Seikh took a deep breath, sighed, and then addressed the Sibyls and his father. "Everyone, we are just a few hundred yards or so away from the Plain of Gemar. We shall make camp here tonight. Try to get some sleep. Tomorrow you will need as much strength as can muster. We will rise at the break of dawn and gather on the west side of Gemar. General Elihu will be bringing more Seers with him from the east. Lamlorde will be coming from the south."

"But we have no weapons and no food!" called out one of the younger Sibyls. "How will we fight or even have the strength to fight?"

"Do not fear!" Seikh responded. "Lamlorde will provide whatever we need."

"Is there a plan we are to follow? How will we know what we are to do?" cried out another.

"Lamlorde has not given me any further commands other than to lead you to the west side of Gemar." Seikh detected some discontented grumbling. "We must trust Lamlorde! The battle belongs to him!"

"He is correct! Listen to him!" Anna confirmed. "The Speech has been with us and guided us through the last several *hundred* years and has *never* abandoned us. Even when the Scientians were bent on committing genocide, wiping out all the Seers, The Speech protected us. He provided us our stone village and kept us from the hand of Sangoma and his puppet king, Surek. We did not know the plan at that time. We had no knowledge of the future. We had nothing then, and we have nothing now. But we trusted him then, and we will trust him now!"

"So be it!" a voice exclaimed.

"Shall it be so!" another called out.

One after the other, they all agreed. Anna nodded at Seikh, and he returned the respect. They all sat upon the dark, dewy ground to rest. Night had fallen and all was quiet, like the calm before a storm.

Seikh awoke with a jerk, his head snapping forward. The morning light had just begun to lie across the land. It cast eerie shadows of the trees on the ground. There was a stench in the air that was unfamiliar. A slight breeze seemed to be carrying it from the north and east.

One by one, Seikh woke his father, Anna, and the others who had been sleeping soundly. Since there was no food to eat, they all rose and gathered, and Seikh addressed them.

"Today, we will see the devastation of Kosmon. But its demise will ring in, once again, the Ancient Order. The plague will be destroyed along with all who refuse to listen to The Speech and follow the great Lamlorde. Be confident and courageous, not in your power, but in the power of Lamlorde!"

Seikh whisked around, grasped the phanos sword from his sack, and lit it. He yelled, "To Gemar!"

"Gemar!" everyone shouted, lifting their fists in the air. Running eastward toward the plain, the Sybils and Seikh's father leapt and jerked back and forth, dodging the rocks and ruts. As they approached Gemar, Seikh's nose began to tickle and run. His eyes watered. The foul stench in the air had become intolerable. He was nauseated, and he began to get sick. But he kept running, leading the Sybils with as much zeal as he could muster.

Not by my power, but by The Speech!

As they approached the tree line of the Woods of Ebony and began to enter the Plain of Gemar, Seikh spotted Surek's army on the northside. The stench was coming from them. It smelled of death. Sangoma stood alone in front of the towering trebuchets, looking directly at Seikh. Sangoma moved his arms in a circle, and purple dust appeared, and sparks of lightning began to flash. An impenetrable, powerful force burst forth from Sangoma and expanded outward over the entire plain. It struck Seikh, his father, and the Sybils like a concrete wall, knocking them to the ground.

"We are ready to destroy you, oh chosen one, and your followers!" Sangoma screeched with evil vindictiveness, slowly walking toward Seikh. "By the strength of the Greater Power, Abaddon, Kosmon will be forever mine! I shall be God, and those with me little gods. We shall rule and live by human reason and the heart. And there will be none of you to stop us! We will live and be happy!"

"No, Sangoma!" Elihu's voice bellowed from the east side of the plain. Thousands of Seers stood behind him, all shining brilliantly. Seikh instantly recognized: they were the prisoners from Surek's dungeons. "It is time for the Ancient Order to be reestablished," Elihu called out. "It's time for Lamlorde to bring life. The plague will be destroyed. The cure is here! And the Ancient One will rule infinitely!"

"And where is your alleged mythical creature, Lamlorde?" Sangoma cackled, beginning to move his arms about once again, purple dust appearing.

"No more!" Elihu shouted, throwing his snake-like staff directly at Sangoma's head. The staff sailed through the air, gleaming red and yellow, with the two snakes coming to life and unraveling. Sangoma attempted to use his powers to counter the staff's attack, but the snakes broke through the gale force and wrapped themselves around Sangoma's neck, strangling and forcing him to the ground with a shriek.

Surek's army erupted in loud shouts. Seikh looked to his left at the thousands of Scientians, Transmutants, and other Kosmonians who had joined Surek. From the midst of the army came rushing a brigade of Scarlet Riders, screeching and armed with glowing golden rods. Just behind them stood Pravitas, arming the trebuchets. Then Surek bolted out from behind them. He did not look kingly as he did in his castle, but as he had in the City of Petra when he killed Elihu. He was mounted on his horse. His long, sleek, slithering tongue protruded from underneath the hood that shielded his face.

Seikh's heart raced, as he looked around the plain in panic. The battle had begun, but where was Lamlorde? He looked to the south. He was not there.

Where is he?

The thought repeated in his mind like a mantra.

Sangoma was back on his feet again, having pulled free from the two snakes. He was conjuring another force to throw at them. Seikh was terrified. He felt something tickling his arm. He looked down to swat it.

It's a tree limb! The trees are coming alive!

Sangoma was conjuring the trees to fight on his behalf. Seikh's eyes looked to and fro at the trees surrounding the plain. They were shaking and beginning to lift their roots to walk.

Without warning, a voice thundered, "Enough!"

Surek's army ceased. The trees immediately stood still. Quiet fell across Gemar. On the south of the plain stood Lamlorde, the donkey, alone, with his head low and his eyes looking dejected.

Sangoma turned and looked at him. "And who might you be, you feeble-minded brute?"

In a soft, sorrowful voice, the donkey said, "I am."

"You are what?" retorted Sangoma wryly.

"I am Lamlorde."

"What?" Sangoma chuckled. "You? Lamlorde?" He chuckled some more. "So you are real! But a feeble donkey!" He laughed uncontrollably. The others chimed in until the entire plain was howling and hooting.

Lamlorde lifted his head slowly and then spoke with force and strength, "Sangoma! Come here!" His voice penetrated and hushed the crowd.

"Why, by all means, you imbecilic beast!" He responded, walking slowly toward him and beginning to conjure another force to deal him a blow.

Lamlorde sat down on his hind legs. And then stretching them upward, he stood up like a Kosmonian. Numerous circles of red, yellow, and gold light began to spiral and whirl around him, changing his appearance. A white luminosity burst from within him, and he took the form of what looked like a Seer. His clothing was white as the City of Light, and his Seerean robe reached the ground. There was snow white, glistening hair on his head that flowed down his back. He had a beard just as white, but he had no hair around his eyes or on his hands. Rather he had skin of dark sienna. His eyes were red, golden flames of fire.

As everyone stood gazing at Lamlorde in awe, he opened his mouth and a two-edged phanos sword protruded from it. In a flash, the sword shot straight into Sangoma's chest with a sound of thunder. Sangoma fell to the ground dead and exploded into ash. Seikh, his father, and all the Seers erupted in cheers. A legion of Seers, radiating as the sun, appeared behind Lamlorde. As Seikh scanned them, he recognized family and friends he once knew as a small child.

Just as quickly as the Seers had appeared, another sword protruded from Lamlorde's mouth, darting through the air and piercing Surek through the heart with a sound of thunder, destroying him. Another sword appeared in Lamlorde's mouth, and another after that one, annihilating the Pravitas, the Scarlet Riders, and all those who were in league with Surek, one right after another until they were all killed. With one final resounding shout, Lamlorde silenced the trees and all his enemies.

In a firm, deep voice, Lamlorde called out, "Abaddon!"

A dense brown and black fog began swirling just a few yards in front of Lamlorde. Appearing with only a black cloak, with no arms, hands, legs, or feet, was Abaddon. He appeared to be kneeing to Lamlorde. Without a word, Lamlorde breathed on him, and Abaddon was set ablaze. A substance that looked like hot lava dripped and clumped up onto the ground. The lava oozed until Abaddon had been entirely consumed by the fire. The mound of lava cooled and then was entirely vaporized.

Seikh stood in shock.

A narrow beam of sunlight peeked through the clouds. It was so unusual that everyone looked up to the sky in astonishment. Slowly, more beams glittered through the clouds. Golden rays filled the Plain of Gemar until every cloud dissipated, giving way to clear skies the color of brilliant azure. Seikh had been so fixated on the dazzling sunlight that he had not noticed the craggy ground had transformed into a feather-soft, green, grassy plain. The trees were no longer dark and dead. They had beautiful leaves that twinkled like emeralds, and their bark was like mahogany. The air was clean and pure. Everything was luminous and alive. The plague of Kosmon—death and the ego—was no more.

Epilogue

T he banquet table, garnished with the most exquisite decor and succulent food, stretched from infinity to infinity. Candelabras of pure
gold, with their wicks lit but their flames dimmer than the light gleaming
from all around the banquet hall, adorned the center of the table. They
stood upon the whitest and most pure cloth ever seen. A powerful and
invigorating aroma of meat, vegetables, and fruit filled the air.

It is a feast fit for kings and queens, Seikh thought joyfully.

Seikh recognized the view: it was the vision he had had back in the
world of Kosmon in the little log cabin. This time, however, it was not a
vision, not a dream. It was real.

Really real.

And this time, it was much more enthralling than one could explain.

All who sat around the beautiful table told stories, laughed, and consumed the food. Their voices filled the air like soft notes from stringed
instruments. Animosity, sorrow, fear, and darkness were nowhere to be
found on their faces. In fact, all their faces, including Seikh's, had been
changed by Lamlorde just after the battle at Gemar. Indeed, the very *nature*
of the remaining Kosmonians had been changed. The Book of Zoe had
been opened by Lamlorde's command, and the light of it shone throughout
Gemar, alighting upon them. Everyone was given skin of dark sienna and
bodies—of arms, legs, and much more—all the same. There were no longer
Scientians, Transmutants, or Seers. There was only one type of beings: the
Ancients. And they shined with the light of Lamlorde.

Seikh had been so preoccupied by the events since the last battle that
he had forgotten all about the world of Kosmon and its troubles. Of course,
Kosmon and the plague were no more. After Lamlorde had defeated Abaddon, the City of Light and the Infinite enveloped and entirely consumed
Kosmon, changing darkness to light. The sun shone so brilliantly that it

was said to be more glorious than it had been long ago before the Ancient Order of old.

The plague of Kosmon—death and pride—was wiped away, and no thought of it remained until Elihu approached Seikh as he was about to take his seat at the table. Beside Elihu stood a lovely lady with long hair and blazon dark sienna skin. Her eyes danced and her posture was one of peace.

"Seikh, my boy!" Elihu exclaimed, patting Seikh on his back with a thud and almost knocking him over.

"Elihu!" Seikh chuckled. "You've got to stop doing that!"

"Well, get some muscle, eh?" Elihu laughed.

"And who is this lovely lady standing next to you?" inquired Seikh.

"Why, I think you might be most surprised and overjoyed!" He placed his arm around her shoulders. "Seikh, my boy, this is your mother, Lucy."

Seikh gazed at her in shock, but with a smile on his face. He lunged at her, wrapping his arms around her neck. "Mom!" Tears of joy welled up in his eyes. "But how?"

"Oh, my son!" she sniffled as tears streaked down her face. "I finally did it. I passed through! I trusted in Lamlorde to cure me, to kill my ego!"

"But father said you died in his arms, looking ghastly as ever."

"Oh, that I did and that I was!" She wiped the tears from her face. "But what your father did not know is that I had passed through back at the castle a few days earlier. Surek had put me in the dungeons. But because I was weak and the dungeons were so full, Surek had Philo lead me into the woods and leave me to die. That's when your father found me, but I couldn't speak because I was so weak. But here I am!"

"Oh, Mother!" Seikh blurted out. "And lovely you are! You have been changed!"

"Yes, she has!" came a very familiar voice. "And we all have been changed! Look! No more limp!" Seikh's father cried out, rejoicing and dancing.

"Father!" Seikh called out in jubilation, hugging both his parents.

"Excuse me, friends," Elihu spoke in his deep voice, "I really hate to interrupt this joyous occasion, but I think Lamlorde is ready for you, Seikh." He nodded toward the table.

Seikh whisked around and there was Lamlorde, just as glorious as he had been at battle.

"General Seikh. Well done!" he clasped his hands upon Seikh's cheeks and then pulled him forward, hugging him. "It's time to take your seat."

Following Lamlorde to the table, Seikh saw a large throne covered with gold and padded with crimson silk. It stood by itself between two other Ancients seated upon smaller thrones.

"Sir, Lamlorde," Seikh spoke humbly, "I don't mean to assume anything or be out of line, but is this throne for me?"

"Yes," Lamlorde replied. "It is your throne. You, along with all the others, will rule the Ancient Order with me."

Slowly and hesitantly, Seikh sat down on the distinguished throne.

"Now eat!" proclaimed Lamlorde.

A sense of peace, contentment, and ultimate fulfillment came over Seikh like a rushing wind. This was his purpose—his meaning! This is what he had been made to be and to do. Purpose had not been found in his rational thought or following his heart. It had been found in denying himself, destroying his ego, and placing his trust in Lamlorde to cure him. It wasn't just for him either; it was for Kosmon.

And so it was finished. The plague had been destroyed, and the Ancient Order restored. Lamlorde ruled alongside The Speech with all the Ancients. Lamlorde had accomplished it all by himself.